Bluegrass Dawn

Bluegrass Single #2

Kathleen Brooks

D1521590

Dedication

A huge "Thank You" to all veterans, their families, and those who support them. All my love to my uncles Marshall and Joe for their service and for sharing their Vietnam experiences with me. And to my parents for teaching me the culture and slang of the '60s and '70s. You're totally far-out.

For all my readers who wrote me asking for Jake and Marcy to have their own story . . . this time in American history was so different from the Keeneston of today that it took me a couple years to write. But I am so glad I did! Thank you for all the support and encouragement you give me. I cherish every Facebook post, tweet, and email.

And finally, to my sweet Megavolt, whom I called Meggy. He was the best horse a kid could have.

DAVIES FAMILY FRIENDS

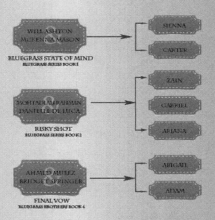

WILL ASHTON
McKENNA MASON

BLUEGRASS STATE OF MIND
BLUEGRASS SERIES BOOK 1

SIENNA

CARTER

MOHTADI ALIBRAHMAN
DANIELLE DE LUCA

RISKY SHOT
BLUEGRASS SERIES BOOK 2

ZAIN

GABRIEL

ARIANA

AHMED MULEZ
BRIDGET SPRINGER

FINAL VOW
BLUEGRASS BROTHERS BOOK 6

ABIGAIL

ADAM

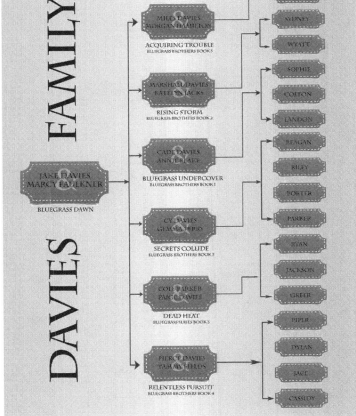

FAMILY

DAVIES

JAKE DAVIES & MARCY FAULKNER

BLUEGRASS DAWN

MILES DAVIES & MORGAN HAMILTON

ACQUIRING TROUBLE
BLUEGRASS BROTHERS BOOK 5

MARSHALL DAVIES & KATELYN JACKS

RISING STORM
BLUEGRASS BROTHERS BOOK 2

CADE DAVIES & ANNIE BLAKE

BLUEGRASS UNDERCOVER
BLUEGRASS BROTHERS BOOK 1

CY DAVIES & GEMMA PERRO

SECRETS COLLIDE
BLUEGRASS BROTHERS BOOK 3

COLE PARKER & PAIGE DAVIES

DEAD HEAT
BLUEGRASS SERIES BOOK 3

PIERCE DAVIES & TAMMY FIELDS

RELENTLESS PURSUIT
BLUEGRASS BROTHERS BOOK 4

LAYNE

SYDNEY

WYATT

SOPHIE

COLTON

LANDON

REAGAN

RILEY

PORTER

PARKER

RYAN

JACKSON

GREER

PIPER

DYLAN

JACE

CASSIDY

Prologue

Keeneston, Kentucky
Spring 1968

M arcy Faulkner wrapped her hands around the cold metal bars of the jail cell and sighed. If her parents found out she had been arrested walking around wet, mostly naked, and in the company of Jake Davies, then she could only pray that the jail bars would protect her from them.

She looked over her shoulder at Jake as he lounged against the cement wall. He was a couple years older than she was and boy, what a difference those years made! Jake was already a man in every sense of the word. He stood well over six feet tall. He had dark brown hair and deep hazel-green eyes that made her feel possessed when he looked at her. His shoulders were broad from working on his family's farm. His legs were muscled and sprinkled with dark hair. And as she noticed during their time swimming in their unmentionables just an hour ago, Marcy knew that the smattering of hair on Jake's sculpted chest tapered into a trail that led straight to his . . . Marcy decided whatever punishment her parents doled out would be worth it.

"Marcy, come sit with me. Old Sheriff Mulford will let us go after we dry off. I cut his grass for him. He's just trying to scare us."

Marcy rolled her eyes and slid her wide headband back into place over her sandy blond hair. "You punched the sheriff in the face, Jake. What were you thinking?"

"That I didn't want our date to end," Jake shrugged. "I didn't punch him hard. Besides, he put us in here together. He's a romantic at heart."

"A romantic with a swollen lip! And what are you talking about? This isn't a date. We went to the prom with different people."

Jake grinned and his eyes danced with a mixture of pride and mischief. "Yeah, but it's who you leave with that counts."

Marcy walked across the cell and sat down a foot away from the man she'd had a crush on for what seemed like forever. She ran a nervous hand down her dress. She had made it for her prom since her mother refused to spend money on a fancy dress. It was a long, satin, baby-blue empire dress with a white-flowered lace overlay.

She cast a quick glance at Jake. How did he seem so comfortable and unconcerned? Tonight had been anything but smooth. Jake's date ditched him for Marcy's date. Marcy hit Jake in the back of the head with a cheese ball, they'd danced the night away, and then snuck out to the pond for a little swim. She had worn her underwear on the way back to their small town of Keeneston not wanting her dress to be ruined. Little did she know that was a crime and by morning everyone in town would know about it. On top of that, the most popular boy in school, Jake Davies, was sitting next to her partially undressed. Sure, she had older brothers and had seen men in various states of undress. But a bare-chested Jake was enough to leave her momentarily speechless.

"Marcy?" Jake asked with a little raise of his eyebrow before patting the bench next to him. "I think we can dispatch with all this nervousness after seeing each other in our drawers. Come sit with me."

Marcy tried to act like it was no big deal, but it was. Her brothers were both away after joining the Navy. And her mother had acted as if she were a great burden since they had left two years ago. Her mother had complained constantly that Marcy was either too young to date, too old to be single, or too stupid to know how to act around boys. It sent her in circles, and as a result Marcy hadn't dated much. It wasn't until her best friend, Betsy Milner, well, Betsy Ashton since marrying her high school sweetheart William after graduating the year before, told Marcy she couldn't get pregnant from kissing that she finally got her first kiss a month ago. But to say it was everything she dreamed of was an overstatement. Instead it had been sloppy and very wet. And now in just a couple of hours, she had gone from being kissed only once to stripping down to swim with a man. Of course, that man hadn't kissed her yet, but she got the feeling he wouldn't drool if he did it.

"I'm sorry," she said as she scooted down the bench. She felt the pant leg of his tuxedo brush against her long skirt and leaned closer wanting to feel more of him. "I've just never done anything like this before."

"I know," he chuckled.

"You do?"

"Sure. Everyone knows about the saintly Marcy Faulkner. She volunteers her time putting together baskets to send the Keeneston men serving in Vietnam, she makes lap robes for the elderly, and she tutors freshmen. But, what I also know is that when I look at you I see even more."

"You do?" Marcy stammered.

3

"You're so passionate about others that you've failed to let yourself have fun. And I'm just the guy to make sure you come out of that shell and live life to the fullest." Jake grinned again and Marcy felt her insides melt. "See, in one night with me you ended up in jail. I can't wait to see what we do next."

"Next? You want there to be a next? What about Mary Donna? She's the queen bee of the Belles." The Keeneston Belles were an invitation-only group of girls who worked to nab the most successful and handsome men in town. They disguised their objectives by pretending to be charitable socialites. Once they nabbed the richest and most desirable men, they moved up into the Keeneston Ladies group and organized garden tours and other society events.

"What about her? We broke up. I was going to do it weeks ago, but she already had her dress and that's just not something a gentleman would do."

"But we don't even know each other." Marcy slammed her mouth shut. Why was she trying to talk him *out* of dating her?

"I knew the second that cheese ball hit my head that you were different." Jake reached out and clasped her hand in his. "See, I'm turning eighteen this September and it's time I start thinking about my future. High school has been groovy, but I'll start working full time on my parents' farm after graduation in June. I'm looking for something more than a Keeneston Belle who wants to pin me down and run roughshod over me with social events and preening. I'm looking for someone with a head on her shoulders, a great aim, and a secret wild streak."

"Me?"

"Do you see anyone else in this cell? But what about you; what do you want? What's your story?"

4

Marcy was so surprised she didn't know what to say. Her mother had sat her down after her disastrous date with the drooler and told her that she wasn't getting any younger. Sure, she was sixteen and a woman now, but sometimes the future didn't feel like her own. Her mother was always telling her what to do and mostly what she *couldn't* do. This might have been the first time someone asked what she wanted out of life.

"Well, my older brothers are in the Navy. They enlisted when the draft started for Vietnam. My dad and mom run an insurance company in town but have been talking about moving to the naval base in South Carolina if my brothers decide to stay in the Navy. But I don't ever want to leave Keeneston."

"They wouldn't make you move before you graduate, would they?"

"I don't think so, but my mother has already had the *talk* with me. She didn't say it outright, but I can read between the lines. If I'm not married right out of high school, then I'm going with them when they leave."

"But won't that just force you into accepting the first guy instead of finding the right guy?" Jake asked.

Marcy sighed. That was exactly what she had told her mother. "With the war going on and the shortage of men, I think she's afraid I'll never get married. I think she just wants me off her hands. Her world revolves around my dad and my brothers."

"Do you want to get married?"

"To you?"

Jake laughed and Marcy felt her face flush with embarrassment. "I'd dig it, but I meant in general."

"Oh. Of course I do. But I'd like to marry for love."

Jake stood up and held out his hand to her.

"What are you doing?" Marcy asked as she put her hand in his.

"Asking you to dance."

"Here?"

"Yes, here. You only get one first date. If I haven't convinced you that I'm worth a second one, then I have a feeling our lives will never be the same."

"Who knew Jake Davies was a romantic at heart?" Marcy teased as she stood up.

Jake pulled her into his arms and sent their bodies swaying to the music in their hearts. "Only for you, Marcy Faulkner." Jake lowered his lips to hers and she felt her world shift. She had been right—there was no drool and it was everything she had read about in Betsy's romance novels.

Her body pressed against Jake's and she felt his arms tighten around her. She felt safe, precious, and sexy all at once. Now *this* was a kiss.

Jake pulled away slowly. "So tell me, Marcy. Would you like to go out with me tomorrow night?"

"I'd love to, Jake," Marcy said a little breathlessly.

The door to the jail opened and the sheriff sauntered in with keys. The best day of her life was coming to an end. She smiled as Jake led her out of the jail cell. Someday she'd tell her grandchildren about this day.

Chapter One

Keeneston
December 1, 1969

J ake Davies took the porch stairs two at a time. The cold weather caused him to shiver, or it could have been his nerves. Tonight was going to change the rest of his life. He just hoped it changed for the better.

He rapped his hand on Marcy's front door and waited for her mother to answer. After dating for over a year and a half, they had developed a routine of sorts. He'd finish working on the farm and then he would wash up and go to the Faulkner house. Sometimes they ate dinner together. Sometimes he took Marcy to the new Blossom Café for a milkshake. Sometimes they'd sit at the pond and he'd just hold her.

The door opened and Mrs. Faulkner opened the door with a worried look on her face. "Good evening, Jake. How are you?"

"I'm fine, thank you."

Mrs. Faulkner was plump with graying hair and little glasses perched on the end of her nose. Her eyes darted around as she twisted her apron. "It's such a shame what they are doing to you young boys. The tension on the news — I can't wait for this war to be over."

Jake tried to relax, but as he walked inside he found the television already on and the news reporter outlining the upcoming events. His stomach plummeted as he wiped his sweaty hands on his jeans.

"How is your mother handling it? She's more than welcome to come watch. I know you don't have a television."

"Thank you, ma'am. My mother said she didn't want to know. I think she'll sneak into the kitchen and listen to the radio, though."

"Jake!" He looked up and saw Marcy racing down the stairs. Her shoulder-length hair was flipped up at the end and held back from her face with a wide black headband. Her short skirt made her mother shake her head. But it made Jake smile. He loved the short skirts she wore with tights and knee boots.

Gosh, he loved her. They had been inseparable since their night in jail. They had been through the death of his father, and then two of their friends from high school during the Vietnam War. They had talked about life after the war and after she graduated high school in six months. He had already talked to her father and received permission to ask her to marry him. He just needed to find the perfect time to propose.

Marcy grabbed his hand and pulled him to the couch. "I can't believe they are doing this. All these men fighting and now they're doing a lottery — why, Father James is even thinking he'll have to leave the church to help provide comfort and guidance to the troops. And did you know Jimmy White was injured? Norma said he might have lost the use of his right arm."

Jake gulped and nodded. He'd heard about Jimmy. John Wolfe had told him yesterday, but he hadn't wanted to worry Marcy. Every morning he would run into John at the Blossom Café when he delivered fresh eggs and bacon to Daisy Mae and Violet Fae Rose, the owners of the Blossom Café. The café had turned into the town hub as soon as it opened on Main Street in Keeneston.

The quaint town had been founded back in the days when Kentucky was the western frontier of America. It had kept its small town charm even as larger cities grew up around it. Flags flew on every light pole, windows sparkled, flowers bloomed, and in the winter garland and white Christmas lights lined the street.

"But, I'm sure you're going to be fine. I mean, there are 365 days of the year. What are the chances your birthday will be drawn early enough in the draft lottery that you have to go overseas?" Marcy was trying to sound positive, but he could hear the worry in her voice.

"Congressman Pirnie is representing the United States Military Affairs Committee . . ." the voice of an old man with white hair and big, thick glasses said as the equally old congressman stepped in front of the cameras. So, these were the men deciding the fate of America's youth.

Marcy fell silent and Jake gripped her hand for support as he kept his eyes on the clear bowl of little blue balls that were about to change the lives of every man in America.

"We are going to ask him to choose the first one . . ." the head of the Selective Service committee said as the congressman stepped forward and reached his hand into the bowl. His hand grabbed many balls, but they dropped back into the bowl until only one small blue ball remained clutched in his fingers. He handed it off and another man cracked the ball like an Easter egg and pulled out a piece of tightly rolled paper.

Marcy squeezed his hand and Jake leaned forward as

the camera kept a steady image of the man's hands unrolling the paper with the first birthdate on it.

"September 14th" the man called out.

There was a collective gasp and Jake felt his stomach drop. He'd just been drafted. He was to report in one month for service.

Marcy felt tears pressing on her eyes. She had to be strong. She couldn't believe it. They were so happy and now he was being forced to leave to fight in this pissing contest of a war. No, she wasn't going to be bitter. It wasn't Jake's fault or any of these young men being forced to serve. She needed to keep a brave face and make sure he and the rest of the boys over there knew they were loved and supported back home.

"I can't believe it," Jake mumbled as he sat rigid next to her.

"You can enlist and serve four years like my brothers. They had the ability to go into another branch of the military and have less of a chance ending up in the jungle."

"Come on, Father, let's let these two have some time together," Mrs. Faulkner whispered as she pulled her husband from the room.

"What do I know about fighting? Killing? I guess I will have to learn and learn quickly."

"Jake, no matter what happens, I will be waiting for you here. I will love you forever and you will come back to me." Marcy threw her arms around his neck and felt him slowly loosen up as she gripped him for all she was worth.

"I can't ask you to do that, Marcy. I could be gone for two years or I could be gone forever. You're young, beautiful, and smart. You shouldn't put your life on hold for me while I go off to fight this war. It's not fair of me to ask that of you."

Marcy fingered Jake's class ring that hung on a necklace around her throat. "You're not asking me. I'm telling you. I love you and nothing will change that."

"But, marriage, children, a house of your own . . . you're giving that all up to be with me?"

"I'm not giving it up. I'll have all of that with you because you will come back to me."

Marcy saw the panic in his eyes. She saw Jake trying frantically to come to terms with his new future.

"The fourteenth birthday in the draft is April 11th," the voice said on television.

Marcy saw Jake whip his head around and look at the television. "What? What is it?"

"That's William Ashton's birthday. It looks as if there will be several of us from Keeneston leaving next month."

"And there will be women who love you who will pray for you and wait with open arms for you to come home safe."

Jake shook his head. "I need to go. I'm sorry, Marcy. I need to process this somehow. I'll see you tomorrow after school, okay?"

The hardest thing Marcy had ever done was to rise up on her tiptoes and place a gentle kiss on his cheek. "Whatever you need, Jake. I'll always be here for you."

Chapter Two

M arcy descended the gray concrete stairs of the Keeneston High School with her arms wrapped tightly around her books. She had hoped school would be a diversion to the dark thoughts running through her head, but it only made them worse.

She hadn't slept the night before due to her worry, and it seemed the draft was all they could talk about in school. Many brothers, cousins, neighbors, and friends had been drafted. In all, ten men from their small town were involuntarily leaving in a month to begin the process of deployment. Another fifteen men had already volunteered or were going to volunteer to avoid being drafted.

"Marcy! Oh, my gosh, I heard about Jake and had to see you." Betsy Ashton slammed the door to her powder blue Mustang and rushed up the stairs. Marcy was wrapped into a hug before she could even say hello to her best friend.

"Oh, Betsy. I'm so glad you're here. I'm so sorry about William."

"At least they will be over there together. I feel better about that." Betsy wiped a tear from her eye and dragged Marcy down the stairs. "We have to stick together and help each other out. I have to learn how to run his farm before he leaves next month. What do I know about breeding and training race horses?"

"Betsy, you'll have those horses running faster than they ever did just to get a scratch on the nose from you," Marcy laughed. Betsy had such a good heart that you couldn't help but fall in love with her.

Betsy laughed and squeezed Marcy's arm. "I sure hope so. Now, how are you doing?"

Marcy let out a long breath. "Every time I close my eyes I see him lying in the jungle . . ."

"Oh, Marcy!" Betsy enveloped her in another hug and let her cry. Normally Marcy would be embarrassed. Having grown up with two tough-as-nails brothers, crying meant she just got picked on more. But she held nothing back at the thought of losing the love of her life. "We'll have each other and we can do anything if we work together."

Marcy gave a sniffle and nodded as she wiped the tears from her eyes. "You're right. We have to be strong and show them every day what they have to look forward to upon return. No more tears until they leave."

"I have to go meet William at the farm and learn the stud book." Betsy shot her a wry grin. "It's not nearly as interesting as you would think."

Marcy couldn't stop the giggle that came out and soon they were laughing together. Only her best friend could make her smile at a time like this. As Marcy watched Betsy hurry back to her Mustang, she wondered how she was going to hide her misery and fear from Jake.

Jake tossed the bales of hay to the top of the stack. Over and over again, he picked up rectangular bale after rectangular bale and carried them to the back of the barn to stack them neatly. Even though it was cold out, he'd shed his coat and

rolled up the sleeves on his flannel shirt. He had to think
about the future and stacking hay helped him think. No
longer could he think of a happy life married to Marcy.
Now it was how many bales of hay his mom would need to
get them to spring on her own. How to teach her to plow
the fields in the spring and how to plant the vegetables they
would need.

He had talked to Mr. Tabernacle, their neighbor down
the road, and Tabby agreed to help as much as he could. He
was too old for the draft but was supporting the troops in a
different way. He was going to help all the families that
were left behind. William told Jake that Tabby was going to
check on Betsy every other day and help her keep the farm
running smoothly. And Jake knew that his mother would
appreciate having him stop by for dinner every now and
then just so she wouldn't have to be alone.

But what about Marcy? She would be alone. She had
her parents, but that wasn't a lot in her world. After being
together the past year, Jake came to realize her mother was
anything but supportive. Jake wrapped his leather-clad
hands around the twine and lifted the hundred-pound bale
and carried it to the back of the barn. The thought of Marcy
being left behind to be romanced by all the men who had
somehow escaped the hell caused by the draft sent the bale
of hay flying through the air. Images of Marcy alone also
filled his mind. Could he ask her to wait for him? The guilt
tore at him because he knew he could never just give her
up.

Marcy sat and stared at her parents. Moving! They were
moving. How could they do this to her? "Your brother Scott

is getting married before he ships out. He wants us there to help with his new wife," her mother stated as she folded laundry.

"But what about me?" Marcy cried. "I'm graduating in six months. And what about Jake? And my friends? And my life here?"

"Stop being so melodramatic, Marcy. You can finish high school in South Carolina. And it's not like Jake will be here waiting for you. He's going to be fighting for his country far away from Keeneston. If Jake hasn't asked you to marry him yet, he's not going to. Plus, your brother Kevin says he has a lot of friends dying to meet you. You're not getting any younger, you know."

Marcy felt like stomping the ground if it hadn't just fallen out from underneath her. "Mom! How can you even suggest that? You know I'm with Jake."

Her mother let out a long breath and sat down on Marcy's twin bed. "Dear, we need to talk about that. He's been drafted and if he goes overseas, you know there is a good chance he's not coming back. It's better to move on with your life now while you have these good memories."

"No. I refuse to toss him aside because of this draft. If he dies over there . . ." Marcy paused and took a deep breath to control her emotions. "If he dies over there, it will be with the knowledge that I'm here supporting and loving him."

"I hate to do this, Marcy, but you've left me no choice. You're coming, end of discussion. We leave after school lets out for Christmas." Her mother stood and picked up the basket of laundry. "You better talk to Jake and let him know. Then I expect you to come home and start packing. You forget you have two brothers serving and they deserve your loyalty."

"But not my life. We've always done everything for them. When have you ever put me first? It's always Scott's football games or Kevin's basketball games. It was never my track meets. Those just got in the way of their games. It was always them!"

"That's a woman's lot in life. It's better you learn it now. Do you think it will be any different when you get married? Then it will be moving for your husband's job and cooking the dinner your husband wants to eat. It's just the way it is and you need to grow up and see that women play an important role in holding the family together," her mother snapped.

"It's not going to be for me. Jake loves me. I'll be happy to cook him whatever he wants, but I'm not going to stop being me either. He would never want me to do that. And if I ever have kids, I'm going to love them all equally. And if I have a daughter, she'll be able to do whatever she wants to with my support!"

Marcy stormed past her mother and ran down the narrow stairs. She paused to grab her coat and to glare at her father.

"Marcy, darling, you need to accept this," he said from over his newspaper.

"And you need to let Mom decide what to make for dinner," Marcy shot back as she slammed the front door.

Chapter Three

J ake was still tossing bales of hay when the door to the barn shuddered with the force of being thrown open. He dropped the bale of hay and looked at Marcy outlined by the cold gray sky. Flurries had begun to fall from the clouds and had dusted her coat.

He pulled off his gloves and dropped them on the hay bale. He knew something was wrong by the way she stood. She was probably here to chew him out for not talking to her sooner. Jake knew he shouldn't have left her out of his decision process, but he needed to make this decision on his own. Luckily, he had gotten out of his own way and he knew he was going to do what his heart had been telling him to do since their one night in jail.

"Marcy. I'm so glad you're here. I'm so sorry," Jake began to grovel before he even reached her.

"Unfair! It's unfair I tell you. They can't make me. They can't!" Marcy screamed in frustration as she slammed the heavy barn door closed.

"What's happened? Are you okay?" Jake grabbed her arms and looked into a tear-stained face.

"No, I'm not okay. My parents are making me move to South Carolina to babysit my brother's new wife."

Jake felt his world fall away. The farm disappeared, the worry of going to Vietnam . . . everything dropped off the face of the earth. "What?"

"My mom just told me," Marcy broke free and started pacing. "We leave January 8th."

Jake dropped onto the bale of hay. He hardly registered the fact that Marcy kept walking back and forth. He couldn't let it happen. He couldn't let her leave. She was sunshine in the darkness of this tense time. She was the only thing that was keeping him going at this point.

"I mean, am I so worthless as to be moved like a pawn just because my brothers want it? Don't I have a say in my own life?"

"Not until you're eighteen."

"One more month," Marcy said with a sigh as she collapsed next to him.

"One more month!" Marcy and Jake said excitedly as they looked at each other.

Jake slid off the bale of hay and onto one knee. He reached into his pocket and pulled out a thin gold band. He had saved money for a year to afford it and had bought it months ago. It was a part of him now, just like she was. Every morning he put it into his pocket hoping that day would be the perfect day to propose.

"I have been waiting for the right time to give this to you, but I realized something earlier today. The perfect time is meaningless. It's the person who matters. I have loved you since you hit me in the head with a cheese ball and I promise you this: I'll never stop loving you. Marcy, will you marry me?"

Jake held his breath. It wasn't the grand romantic gesture he had been trying to pull off, but it was from his heart and that was the important thing. He could see the emotions running wild in her eyes as she stared at the ring he held in his fingertips.

"Can I decide what to make for dinner half the nights?"

That wasn't what Jake had expected her to say. "Of course. If you're cooking, then I don't care what it is. I'll eat it."

"And if we have a girl, will you let her do anything the boys do and treat her equally?"

Jake shook his head. "No. I can't do that." Marcy's face turned pale and he almost laughed. "If we have a little girl, then I'll teach her to shoot, ride a horse, and anything else she wants to do. But I'll also spoil her just a little more."

Marcy launched herself at Jake. She knew they would have the happiest of lives together because they had each other. They could handle her parents and the war, as long as they were together.

He caught her as they fell back against the hay. "Yes! Yes, I'll marry you!" She answered as his arms held her tight. She wanted nothing more than to have a little girl for him to spoil.

Marcy laughed as Jake rolled her onto the hay and claimed her mouth in a celebratory kiss. She didn't care that straw was in her hair or that her parents would probably be relieved to get her off their hands. She didn't care that the possibility of this move was to push Jake in to asking her to marry him. She didn't care that in one month she would marry the man of her dreams and then watch him leave the next day. All she cared about was their love.

"Oh! This is wonderful news!" Marcy's mother clapped her hands and gave her and Jake a hug. Marcy stood stiff as her parents celebrated. It would have been more of a celebration if her parents hadn't been so relieved. It was like they were glad she wasn't going with them to South Carolina.

Her mother then reached into the kitchen drawer and pulled out a list. She handed it to Marcy to read. Marcy had always thought she was grown up, but as her parents started talking about all the things she and Jake needed to do before getting married her head started to spin. There on the piece of paper was a list of things she needed to do before they left next month. She was only seventeen. What did she know about being a wife, running a house, or budgeting? She'd never grocery shopped in her life. She always wrote out a list and her mother got it for her.

Marcy let out a shaky breath as the realization hit her. She'd treated her mother the same way her father had. They had been taking advantage of her for years. No wonder her mother didn't care what Marcy wanted.

"Your brothers will be so happy for you. Of course, they won't be able to make your wedding," her mother clucked as she started tying an apron around her waist.

"Why not?" Marcy asked. "I'm going to Scott's wedding."

"You are?" Her mother asked innocently. "And how are you going to get there? You don't have a car. You don't have any money for a plane ticket."

Marcy felt her mouth fall open. Her parents were leaving the day after Jake shipped out. She had thought she could drive out with them to see her brothers, but obviously she was wrong.

"Mother . . ." her father started, but her mom cut him off.

"No. She's going to be a married woman now. She's no longer our worry. If she wants to see her brothers, then she can find her own way. But it won't matter really. They'll be too busy getting ready for the wedding. They won't have time to occupy a little sister trailing after them."

"Marcy won't be able to go anyway," Jake said with a hardness to his voice. "My mother will be too busy spoiling her rotten. She's always wanted a daughter."

Jake smiled down at her. "Let's go tell Mom the good news."

Marcy gave a distracted nod of her head and let Jake usher her out of the house she'd grown up in. She would never step foot in it again after her wedding. The "For Sale" sign was already in the yard and a good portion of her room was now in boxes.

Jake didn't know what to say. He had had a wonderful relationship with his parents. They had taught him the meaning of hard work, good manners, and family. He knew his mother would welcome Marcy with open arms. Unlike Marcy's parents, his had been older when they had him. They didn't think they would be able to have children. But his mother had gotten pregnant at the age of forty-three. They had showered Jake will all the love and attention a boy needed.

Jake hoped the prospect of a new generation of Davies would cheer his mother up. When his father died of a heart attack the year before, his mother had lost her spark. They had been married for almost forty-four years. The small farmhouse came into view as he drove up the long driveway through the family farm. Someday it would be his. Someday it would be filled with his and Marcy's children. Someday it would be her walking out of the screen door and onto the porch. He hoped that he could expand the house and give her a beautiful wraparound porch where their children would play.

His mother waved a dish towel in greeting before

slinging it over her shoulder. Marcy finally relaxed a bit. "Thank you for earlier, Jake."

"I'd do anything in the world to protect you, Marcy. For now and always, I will love you."

She smiled and his heart melted. He leapt out of the old truck and hurried around the hood to open the door for his fiancée. "Mom! I have some exciting news."

His mother smiled and he felt time roll back. She was happy again. "I can't wait to hear it. Come inside and tell me. I just made an apple pie."

"You have to teach me how to make it," Marcy smiled as she slipped her arm around his mother. "I love your apple pie. And your fried chicken."

"If this news is what I'm hoping, we'll have plenty of time for me to teach you everything I know."

Chapter Four

M arcy sat on her bed with a pen and circled the only "help wanted" ad in the *Keeneston Journal*. The end of the semester had taken up all of her time. The spare time she did have was spent making her own wedding dress. Now she only had a week until she was to be married and she needed to find a job and a place to live. Jake's mother, Helen, had told her she could stay with her. But Marcy wanted to stand on her own two feet. So they'd reached an arrangement that pleased them both. While Marcy finished high school, she would live with Helen and work after school. She'd save money and find a place of her own after graduation. If only she could get that job.

The bell to the cheery Blossom Café rang as Marcy stepped through the door. The place was full of high school kids getting milkshakes and burgers after school. Marcy smiled and waved at her friends as she stood looking for the owners.

"Can I help you, hon?"

Marcy turned and saw Daisy Mae Rose standing with a pad in her hand and a pen stuck in her long, straight mahogany hair. She wore a sheath dress covered in large daisy flowers, green tights, and black knee-high boots.

"Hi, Daisy Mae. I don't know if you remember me, but

I'm Marcy Faulkner."

"Sure do. You're the lucky broad who nabbed Jake Davies. I hear congratulations are in order. What can I do for you?"

"Um. I've come to apply for the waitress job you advertised for," Marcy said quietly as some of the kids from school looked on.

"Don't you have school?"

"Yes, but I can work the after-school and dinner shifts. I can start next week. The wedding is on Friday and Jake leaves Saturday morning."

Daisy Mae tapped the pad with one finger as she thought. "And your parents leave for Charleston on Saturday as well. That's a lot of change in your life right now."

"How did you know about that?"

"Honey, I know everything that goes on in this town. You wouldn't believe what the customers talk about over their milkshakes and fries. Anyway, my sweetie Robert is over in Vietnam so I'll give you the job. Women of soldiers need to stick together. Violet!" Daisy screamed out.

"Hold on. I don't want to burn this pecan pie," Marcy heard Violet shout from the kitchen.

"Come meet my sister. She's the cook in the family. My other sister, Lily Rae, just started a bed-and-breakfast in the house we grew up in."

Marcy smiled. They'd heard all about Miss Lily's new place. Apparently she was rather strict with manners even though she was a known flirt. Marcy's classmates couldn't get over how uptight she was. They just wanted "love" . . . with anyone. Miss Lily wouldn't allow single people of the opposite sex to stay on the same floor. She also wouldn't allow drugs or hippies. Not that Keeneston was overrun with either, but the few in town were definitely not *diggin'* her rules.

"Violet Fae, meet our new waitress, Marcy Faulkner. Well, by the time she starts working next week, she'll be Marcy Davies."

Violet Fae's shapely round bottom was up in the air as she bent over to pull her pies from the oven. Violet was the opposite of Daisy. Where Daisy was tall and svelte, Violet was short and curvy. Men overseas would be posting pictures of her ample assets all over their barracks. Her hair was lighter than Daisy's — more golden like her sister, Lily.

"That's wonderful! Lord knows we need the help. We had no idea this place would take off like it did." Violet put the pies on the counter and slid two French silk pies into the oven. "Did you tell her the rules yet?"

"Not yet." Daisy turned to her. "No drugs, no hippies. Same rules my sister Lily has. If the hippies would stop stealing my flowers, then I'd have no problem with them. They've ruined my garden with all their 'flower power.' Show up on time and if a customer gets grabby," Daisy put a wooden spoon in her hand, "bop them on the head with this. Works every time."

Violet smiled and bobbed her head. "A spatula to the face also works. But the most important rule of all — if you hear any good gossip, you have to tell us."

Marcy went from astonishment to laughter in a split second. The three of them shared a conspiratorial smile. Even though these ladies were older than she was, she knew they'd all become good friends.

"Thank you so much. I need the money to find my own place after I graduate."

"Aren't you going to be staying with Miss Helen?" Violet asked as she sliced her pies.

"Until I graduate. But I want to know what it's like to take care of myself. I have to learn to do my own laundry, pay my own bills, and do my own shopping. I know it sounds crazy, but it's something I have to learn before Jake gets back."

They all ignored the obvious *if* Jake gets back hanging in the air.

"There's a place above the café if you want to rent it from us. We lived there for the past year, but just got our own places as well. We understand what you mean." Daisy smiled and then looked into the seating area.

"Hey, you!" Daisy grabbed her wooden spoon and stalked out of the kitchen. "Stop stealing my flowers!" The sound of a spoon being cracked over the shaggy head of the young man reverberated through the café.

Jake Davies stood tall at the front of Saint Francis in his best black suit as he watched his bride walk down the aisle on the arm of her father. Her white velvet gown had a blue ribbon under her breasts that wrapped around and tied in the back. Trailing behind her was a long veil she'd told him had been her great-grandmother's. She'd talked her mother into allowing her to have the family heirloom instead of her brother's fiancée.

His own mother stood happy in the front row. She'd changed in the past month. Every night she and Marcy made dinner together. She showed her all the old family recipes and even helped her with her gown while Jake prepared the farm for his absence as best he could.

Marcy stopped and her father placed a kiss on her cheek before handing her over to Jake. Father James, the new priest who couldn't have been much older than Jake, started the ceremony. Jake was now responsible for this woman. It settled him. He felt it standing there in church. His life just changed and he'd actually felt it. He felt the maturity slide over him. He felt his chest expand with pride. He had a beautiful wife to care for, a partner in life, and someone to love. Jake experienced a happiness he'd never known as he kissed his new wife.

Marcy looked into Jake's hazel eyes as he lowered his lips to hers. She was married! He looked so handsome in his suit and he'd held her hand through the whole ceremony, letting her know how much he wanted this. His lips met hers and her body tingled in response. Tonight there would be more. Tonight she'd finally become a woman in every single way.

He pulled back and smiled down at her. She smiled back and he ran with her down the aisle. Betsy and the other attendants walked out after them to sign the marriage license.

Before she knew it, they were hurrying out of the church. Rice rained down on them as their friends cheered. Jake opened the door to his truck for her and they waved goodbye to their friends and family. With so little time together, they had decided against a reception. Lily Rae had graciously gifted them her largest room for their one-night honeymoon. Jake had to leave in twelve hours. But Marcy refused to think about it. Instead she had much more pleasant things to think about.

"We're here, Mrs. Davies," Jake grinned as he stopped outside the white Victorian bed-and-breakfast. The rose bushes that were always so beautiful during the summer were now covered in a dusting of snow.

Jake hurried around the truck and opened her door. "Thank you, Mr. Davies," Marcy giggled.

Instead of holding out his hand for her to take, he stepped toward her. In a quick move, he had her out of the truck and into his arms. He kicked the door closed with his foot and carried her to the front porch. His eyes never left her and even someone as inexperienced as she was knew what the extra spark meant.

Lily Rae opened the front door as Jake carried her up the steps. Marcy couldn't tell you what she was wearing or what she said. All her attention was on Jake. She felt Lily shove a key into Jake's hand and maybe some laughter as Jake carried her up the curving staircase to the top floor.

He shifted her in his arms and opened the door. With a solid kick, it slammed shut. When Jake placed her on the large four-poster bed, Marcy didn't need to worry about undressing. The fire in her new husband's eyes would burn any clothes right off of her.

It was still dark when Jake looked down at the bed his new wife was sleeping in. Her hair was wild and spread out in every direction on the white pillowcase. It was the most erotic image he'd ever seen and one that would carry him through this war.

Hell, the whole night would be relived many times over the next two years. He bent over and placed a kiss on her smooth cheek. Two full years apart from her. He didn't know how they were going to do it. He'd just have to learn how to write long letters and was already anticipating the ones she would send him. Those letters and these memories would keep his spirits up.

"Sweetheart, it's time," he whispered as he pushed a lock of hair from her face.

Marcy's eyes shot open. "It can't be," she said sadly. "It's still dark. Surely we have hours left."

"I'm sorry. It's time. William is outside. We're driving down to Fort Campbell together. Betsy's there, too, and will take you to my mom's house."

There was a tightness in his chest that wouldn't go away as he watched her dress. This could be the last time he saw the love of his life. It was almost too much to handle. He gritted his teeth. He wasn't a coward. He wasn't going to shirk his duty. He wasn't going to like it—in fact, it made him mad as hell. But the world was in chaos and it was his turn to do what he could.

Marcy slid naked from bed and stepped into the outfit she'd brought with her. She hung up her wedding dress and Jake helped her get ready in silence. Too soon she was walking outside in the morning darkness. No one spoke. Betsy stood quietly, wrapped in William's arms. Jake similarly had his arm around her as he came to a stop a short distance away from the couple. With a silent acknowledgment between the two men, William turned and started whispering to Betsy.

Jake took his bag and tossed it into the back of William's truck and then placed Marcy's bag in Betsy's car. Marcy stood silently and watched him. Was this going to be the last time she ever saw him? Ever touched him?

As soon as he was in front of her, she ran her hands over his wide shoulders, down his chest, and over his tight abdomen. She willed her fingers to remember every detail as she tried to memorize every aspect of his face—the gold flecks in his eyes, the curve of his jaw, the taste of his lips.

She didn't know what to say so she just kissed him. She

begged him to come home safe with her tongue. She pleaded with him to be careful with her hands. And she told him he was loved with her lips.

And then he was gone.

The sound of the front door opening broke the silent spell she and Betsy were under. They both turned and found the three Rose sisters standing there with tears in their eyes. Lily held out brownies, Daisy held out two boxes of tissues, and Violet held open her arms. Somehow, with the town's help, Marcy and Betsy would survive this. She just prayed their husbands would, too.

Chapter Five

Jake completed the intelligence test and handed it in. William had finished five minutes earlier and was waiting for him outside. They'd made it to Fort Campbell and had taken their physicals. Upon passing, they had been assigned a bunk and then headed to take a string of tests. If they passed them all, then they'd start basic training. If they failed, then they would be headed back home.

"How was it?" William asked as they walked to the mess hall.

"Pretty easy. I've heard if you score well enough, you're eligible to enlist in the Navy, Marines, Air Force, or Coast Guard," Jake said as he watched all the men training to be sent overseas doing drills in the distance.

"I'm hoping to join the Kentucky Air National Guard for four years if I can. It will be tough for Betsy to run the farm, but I could maybe be stationed in Kentucky close to the farm. At least I'd be alive. What are you going to do?"

Jake shook his head. "I don't know. Four years seems like a lifetime. But two years in a jungle halfway across the world could mean my life."

"Davies!" Jake turned and saw the recruiter walking his way.

"Good news, I hope. I'll catch you later and you can fill me in," William said as he smacked Jake's shoulder.

"Okay. I'll see you on the flip side." Jake waited for the recruiter. "Yes, sir."

"Have you ever had an IQ test before?"

"No, sir."

The recruiter looked through the file he was carrying. "You're a farmer?"

"Yes, sir."

"Ever been to college?"

"No, sir. We couldn't afford it, especially after my father passed away."

"Only child?"

"Yes, sir."

The recruiter slammed the file shut. "Are you looking to volunteer?"

"I don't know, sir. I just got married and four years seems a long time to be away. But fighting in a jungle doesn't hold that much appeal either."

"I looked over your test before it went off to be officially graded. I saw enough to know you have one of the highest test scores we've seen, especially in strategy. Come to my office today at five. I may have a win-win for you, your new wife, and the Army."

"Yes, sir."

Jake stood staring at the officer walking away. What could that mean? He guessed he'd find out soon enough.

Marcy set the plate of fried chicken down in front of John Wolfe and smiled. He was a nice man. He'd gotten married about five years ago. His wife was a teacher at the middle school.

"Here you go, Mr. Wolfe."

"Thank you, darlin'. I heard Jake and William are doing well down at Campbell."

Marcy felt the blood drain from her face. He'd been gone just a day and a half and she had never felt more alone. "How do you know that?"

Mr. Wolfe winked. "I have my sources."

Marcy narrowed her eyes. "Are they reliable sources?" Mr. Wolfe just raised an eyebrow. "Will you keep me up to date on Jake and William if I bake you my mother-in-law's famous apple pie?"

"I would do it for nothing, but I'm not one to turn down pie," Mr. Wolfe laughed as his broad shoulders shook. He rubbed his long brown sideburns and smiled up at her. "I hear he's going to get some good news tonight. Let me know how it goes tomorrow."

Marcy gave a shaky nod and hurried back into the kitchen to tell Daisy and Violet. Maybe they had some insight they could share on this source.

"No one knows," Violet said with a shrug.

"But it gets my goat," Daisy muttered. "In high school, he knew everything. I could never beat him to the news. But it bothered Lily even more. So I don't know, Marcy. However, I can tell you he's nearly always right."

"Then that's good, right?" Marcy asked excitedly.

"It's very encouraging," Violet said with a wide smile.

Jake knocked on the officer's door and waited for permission to enter. When he stepped into the room, he saw a high-ranking officer standing along with his recruiter.

"Davies," he said. "I'm Major General Noble."

Jake shook the older man's hand. "Nice to meet you,

sir."

"I've seen your IQ test results. You have a good mind for strategy."

"Thank you, sir." Jake wasn't sure where this was going, but it had to be important for a major general to be here.

"I have a small unit over in Vietnam. They are in charge of assisting the commanders in developing military strategy. The group is a mix of the different branches. There's a man each from the Navy and Air Force, along with three from the Army. I want you in this group. Before you decide if you're going to join the puddle pirates in the Coast Guard, I want to give you some more information."

"Yes, sir?" Jake asked. Apparently what he'd heard was right. He'd gotten high enough test scores to get into the very desirable Coast Guard if he wanted to serve four years.

"If you sign on with me, you'll have the opportunity to become an officer if you prove yourself. You'll serve two years and you won't be on the front lines. You'll still be in Vietnam and there will still be danger, but you'll be at our headquarters. You have a strong mind, boy, and I want to use it."

"Two years?" Jake asked again. He would still be overseas, but at least he wouldn't be in the jungle.

"Two years. And I'll see what I can do about getting you a phone call or two with your new wife while you're over there."

Jake held out his hand. "Deal."

"Officer Davies," William chuckled. "I can't believe it — and only two years. Man, who knew you were so smart?"

"I'm not an officer yet and I don't know. I was okay in school, but I guess all that time planning out the crops and harvest came in handy."

"And all those years hunting with your dad."

Jake agreed. His father had had a way of pointing things out that most people couldn't see — a trail, a plan, the way things worked. He taught Jake to never just look at one thing, but to look at the whole picture. In this case, his dad might have just saved his life.

"What about you? Did you find out your results yet?" Jake asked.

"I scored high enough to get into the Kentucky Air National Guard. I decided to take it. It's four years, but I can work my way into a post in central Kentucky and then I'd be less than an hour from home. I'd be able to get to the farm some and I'll be able to call Betsy every week."

"Isn't the Guard on active duty?"

"Yeah. There's a chance I could see you overseas. But with all the trouble on college campuses, there's an equal chance the governor will keep us in state."

Jake raised his soda and they clinked their glasses together in the mess hall. "To my army assignment and to you getting into the Kentucky Air National Guard. May it see us safely home to our beautiful wives."

"Hear! Hear!"

Chapter Six

January 1971

M arcy closed her eyes and blew out the deep breath she had taken. *I wish for Jake to come safely home to me.* She opened her eyes and saw her friends clapping. Helen slid the birthday cake away from where Marcy had just blown out her nineteen candles and started cutting it up.

All of her friends sat around the kitchen table in the small farmhouse. Betsy smiled and handed her a present. "Thank you, Betsy. You didn't have to get anything for me." They had been each other's rock through this past year. William had been sent to quell riots at college campuses within the state but, luckily, had not been sent overseas. Sweet, bubbly Betsy had grown up as she took the reins to the farm.

So had Marcy for that matter. Helen had taught her everything she knew about farming, family traditions, and cooking. Marcy worked the farm from sunrise to eleven in the morning and then served lunch and dinner at the café. She's been busy running herself into the ground in hopes of passing time quickly. But it still seemed an eternity from when Jake was going to be coming home. She'd get letters from him once a month. They usually came in large bundles. She would allow herself to read only one a day so she never had to go long without hearing from him.

Marcy tore into Betsy's package and held up a ticket. "It's a ticket to the Kentucky Derby," Marcy gasped.

"A horse I trained is most likely going to run and I can't think of anyone I would want to go with more than you. It'll be far-out."

"Oh, that sounds fab!" Lily Rae clapped. The Rose sisters had become more like older sisters to her during the past year. They supported her, loved her, and even let her sneak into the kitchen to cry when bad news hit the town. So far, two of Keeneston's own were not coming home.

Everyone lived in fear of Father James and a member of the military coming to see them. One day the priest and a representative of the Army came into the café and Marcy nearly collapsed. Instead, they were there for the parents of one of her classmates. Marcy had stood frozen as she watched the news being delivered and prayed harder than she'd ever prayed before for Jake to remain safe.

Although Jake couldn't tell her anything about where he was, he did tell her he was mostly safe. He'd managed one phone call so far about five months ago. They'd had two minutes. She still replayed that short conversation over and over again in her head.

John Wolfe had told her Jake's unit was being moved closer and closer to the front lines. While he would not be out in the jungle fighting, his unit was helping the commander determine strategy and send out parties of elite soldiers and were instrumental in planning the destruction of several key supply lines.

Just at that moment, John flung Helen's front door open and ran into the small living room.

"What in tarnation?" Daisy asked as everyone stared at John.

"Phone," he panted. "Jake is going to call any minute. He only gets a few minutes."

Everyone erupted in movement. The cake was picked up off the table and set on the counter. A pad of paper and a pencil were placed in front of Marcy in case she wanted to write down anything he said. Presents were moved and then they all left the kitchen just as the phone rang.

Marcy grabbed it before the first ring was finished. "Jake?"

"How did you know? I was hoping to surprise you for your birthday."

"John told me. How are you? Where are you? Are you safe?"

Jake chuckled over the phone and Marcy felt tears start to trail down her cheeks.

"I'm fine. I can't tell you where I am. I'm safe for now. How are things there? How are you? What are you wearing?"

Marcy sobbed and laughed at the same time. "I'm good. I've saved up a nice nest egg. The apartment over the café is perfect for me still. Your mother gave me a new photo from our wedding to hang up as a birthday present. The farm is doing well. We have everything ready for the spring and the cows are nice and fat."

"I guess I should also say happy early anniversary. One year. We made it, sweetheart. Do you regret it?"

"Not one moment. Marrying you was the best thing I've ever done."

"You didn't answer my earlier question. Are you wearing one of those cute short skirts and tights?"

Marcy laughed again. "You know me so well. Red wool skirt with black buttons up the middle and black tights. And those knee-high boots you like so much."

"God, I can't wait to get back to you. I have to go, sweetheart. I love you so much."

"Wait!" Marcy cupped her hand over the phone and called for Helen. "Your mom didn't get to talk to you last time. Please, ten seconds. She's been so wonderful."

She heard Jake say something to someone and then he came back. "I got thirty seconds. I'll try to call again in a couple months. I love you, Marcy. I dream of you every night."

"I love you too, Jake." Marcy handed the phone to Helen as her friends wrapped her in their arms and held her as she cried.

Seconds later Helen came out of the kitchen with red eyes. Silently she pulled Marcy into a hug and just held her. "Thank you for letting me tell my son I love him. To hear his voice one more time. Thank you, dear daughter."

Marcy set a plate of country-fried steak down and laughed as John's wife teased him. Everyone was optimistic about the New Year. So far, 1971 had been going strong in Keeneston. The tension and the campus riots hadn't reached their little town. New ribbons had been placed on all the trees for the town's soldiers. Gift baskets had been assembled and sent out to reach them for Valentine's Day, which was now just a week away.

And, to make the day even better, Marcy had received a bundle of love letters from Jake. To read his words of love brought joy to her every day. To read about his day and the men in his group made her feel a part of his life even though she was halfway across the world.

Daisy came up to her and gave her a hip bump. "Got a

new table." Marcy looked around and spotted Reverend Hamilton and his wife come in with their new baby girl, Pam. She started to head over to them when the door chimed as Father James and Sheriff Mulford walked in.

Marcy froze and she felt Daisy move closer to her. But, if it were about Jake, it would be someone from the Army. She let out a breath only to worry why they headed her direction.

"Mrs. Davies, can we have a word in private?" Sheriff Mulford asked quietly.

"Sure, Sheriff," Daisy answered as she pushed a frozen Marcy into the kitchen.

"Don't tell me the Rev has made another request for me to change the way I make my chicken," Violet started before she saw the sheriff and Father James.

Before Marcy knew it, she had a Rose sister on each side. The front door slammed open and Lily sprinted through the restaurant and into the kitchen with her skirt halfway up her thighs. "We're here for you, Marcy. What is it?"

Sheriff Mulford cleared his throat. "I'm real sorry, Marcy . . ."

Marcy would have dropped to the floor if the Rose sisters hadn't caught her. "Jake?" The name came out of her as though it had been ripped from her soul.

"No, it isn't Jake," Father James said softly.

"What?" the four ladies said at the same time.

"I'm real sorry," the sheriff started again. "It's Helen. She's passed away."

"That's impossible," Marcy was standing now and shaking her head.

"I was just out in the pastures feeding the cows with her this morning. She was fine."

Father James approached and took her hand gently in his. "She swore us to secrecy, but Helen has been battling breast cancer for the past year. The doctors told her she only had months, but she swore she'd talk to Jake one more time. She fought with everything she had. Three weeks ago, she saw the doctor and he told her it would happen any day. She called us in and told us. I counseled her and prayed for her. The sheriff and I checked on her every day. Until today."

"What about Jake?"

The door to the kitchen opened slowly and John put his head in the door. "Is it Helen?"

Father James nodded. "I'm so sorry, darlin'," he said to Marcy. "She was a hell of a woman."

John's wife pushed passed the priest and wrapped Marcy in a hug. "It's okay, sweetie. We'll all help you. You won't have to do this alone."

"How am I going to tell Jake his mother died?"

"With John's help, I'll tell him," Father James said softly. John and he shared a look and Marcy knew John would somehow get the young priest on the phone with Jake. She wanted to be there for him, but right now she was lost.

"Come on. Let's get you upstairs," Daisy said gently. Marcy could only nod. She was lost in a world that seemed to be spinning out of control.

She couldn't call her parents. They hadn't spoken since a week after she had gotten married. Her mother didn't think it was worth the money to call long distance. She had gotten a birth announcement from her new sister-in-law she'd never met. Her own brothers hadn't bothered to call or write. They were strangers now. She didn't even know it had happened. Just one day she realized she didn't even know what was happening with them. Where they even still in South Carolina?

But she'd had Helen. Helen had taught her recipes that had been passed down through generations. Helen had taught her how to farm, how to read the weather, and how to talk down an angry bull. No wonder she taught her so much. She wanted to impart the knowledge on the next generation before she passed on. That realization gave Marcy peace, though grief was still hitting her hard. Helen had accomplished everything she needed. She'd secured the next generation with the family history and she'd been able to say goodbye to her son. And just this morning, they had laughed so hard over stories of Jake in his youth that tears had fallen. Yes, Marcy was sad. But she was thankful at the same time.

Funeral arrangements were now being set. People were coming in to see what they could do to help. The small apartment was full of people from town. John made his way in and let her know that Jake had received the news. Unfortunately, with the importance of his position, he wouldn't be able to come home for the funeral.

"He gave us instructions," John said quietly as he handed her a piece of paper. "And he says to tell you he loves you and he wants you to know you have his full support for running the farm."

"He does?" Marcy asked through the haze of grief.

"He does. When I asked about the farm, he said he wasn't worried. He knew you were smart and would excel at running it."

Jake's support warmed her heart and gave her the confidence she needed.

Mr. Tabernacle came forward with a piglet and handed it to her. "Helen was a top-notch woman. I enjoyed every lunch I had with her this past year. She'd talked about having a small pigpen. This is Bertha. She'll make a good start to it. Don't you worry none, Mrs. Davies. I'll help you through this."

Marcy looked up into Tabby's face, tanned from the long hours in the sun, and saw such kindness she almost started crying if it weren't for the piglet squirming in her arms. At that moment, she stopped feeling helpless. She wasn't helpless. She had an entire town supporting her.

"Thank you, Tabby. How about next week? I'll make you lunch and then we'll start working on the pen."

Tabby smiled at her. "Yes, ma'am. And Bertha here likes to sleep under the covers." With a wink, he headed out the door and Marcy found the strength to laugh.

Chapter Seven

Jake felt the sweat rolling down his back in the hot tent. The month of May in the jungle put Kentucky's humidity to shame. Eight months was all he had left until he could get home, but that felt like an eternity. He had talked to Marcy for his allotted two minutes in March. She had moved into the farmhouse and told him everything was fine. How she could say that, he didn't know. Marcy didn't know anything about farming and he tried not to worry about coming home to debt and a ruined family farm.

If anyone could pick up the reins and run a farm, it was Marcy. She was so smart—it was one of the things he admired most about her. That, and she was blessed with a will of sheer determination. If she didn't know how to do something, he bet she wouldn't give up until she'd mastered it. His mother's fried chicken recipe was proof of that. She'd burnt two pans getting it right. But when she did, it was mouth-watering.

Jake had gotten a letter from John that week that had been written a month ago. In it, John assured the young soldier that Helen had thoroughly approved of Marcy as a wife and loved her as if she'd been her own daughter. The town, he said, had been helping Marcy when she needed it. Tabby was over there twice a week and apparently Jake had been replaced in his marital bed by a pig named Bertha. He didn't know what that was about so he made sure to ask Marcy about Bertha in his next letter to her.

"If we move troops here," his commander pointed to a map spread out on the table, "and have bombers hit here, then we may be able to take out the train and nearby ground troops."

Jake tilted his head and looked at the map. Something was off. It was too easy. "I don't think so, sir."

"What is it, Davies?"

"It doesn't seem right. They've hidden their transportation so well. Why would they be so out in the open about transporting missiles?"

"Do you think it's a trap?"

"I do. Look." Jake pointed to the map. "This section of the railroad is surrounded by mountains. Granted, they're not the Rockies, but they would be more than enough to support an ambush."

"And we'd be stuck in a funnel. Good thinking, Davies."

"If you don't mind me saying, we could try something different," Jake started. His commander gave his approval and Jake studied the map. He looked at the topography, the elevations, and the surrounding terrain for a long time. "Here." Jake pointed to the map. "And here. We could outflank them. There's dense jungle for coverage and the elevation would be to our advantage. I say you bomb the mountains that they are most likely hiding in. When they run for cover in the jungle, they have to cross this open area and our troops could intercept them."

The men in the room studied the map and whispered among themselves. His commander tapped the map and grinned. "We could catch them by surprise and we'd limit ground fighting to protect our men. Good job, Davies."

Marcy twirled around in the fanciest dress she had ever seen. "How do I look?"

"Fab!" Betsy laughed as she also twirled around. "What about me?"

"Amazing!" Marcy laughed. The two of them were decked out to the nines for the Derby. Marcy had sold her first round of alfalfa hay. She decided to use the extra money to increase the cattle herd, she cleared one of the backfields on the property, and she'd also planted the tobacco and soybeans. She saved enough by working the dinner shifts at the Blossom Café to buy her beautiful sky-blue dress. She hoped to wear it when Jake came home.

"Do you have any spare money to bet on Meggy?" Betsy asked.

Marcy rolled her eyes. "Why would you call him that? Poor horse, his name is My Megavolt."

"Pish, he likes it. The horse gives me a kiss every day when I watch him train."

Marcy walked over to where Big Bertha, no longer the cute little piglet she was a couple months ago, sprawled. "Up, Big B." The pig gave her a sad look as if she couldn't believe Marcy was actually interrupting her nap on the kitchen rug. Finally Bertha got up and trotted slowly out the open kitchen door.

"What are you doing?" Betsy asked as Marcy kicked the rug away.

"I figure my money is safe under Bertha. She doesn't move for anyone but me." She loosened the floorboard and pulled out a cookie jar. "I saved one hundred dollars. That's how much faith I have in your training ability."

Betsy laughed and pulled out her money. "It's the same

amount of faith as I have," she laughed.

A couple of hours later, they were sitting under the twin spires of Churchill Downs. The infield was filled with free-spirited men and women grooving to the music and cheering on the races. Men and women from every level of society and political beliefs crammed into the racetrack to share their love of horse racing. On this day, the war wasn't discussed. Instead, it was who was going to win — a long shot from the mutuel field or one of the favorites? The flowers adorning the long hair of women were roses in honor of the Derby, instead of flowers of peace. The tension of the world stopped at the gates of Churchill for just one day.

Marcy grabbed Betsy's hand as they raced through the crowd and into the paddock. Meggy stood in his stall with his trainer and jockey. People walked by, taking pictures and cheering on their picks as the other races thundered on the nearby track.

"There he is," Betsy dragged Marcy through security and ran up to her horse to give him a hug. "Mrs. Wyatt has been helping me with the horses. She and Beauford have been so kind to me. They, along with William's mother, have taught me all about racing, training, and breeding. I couldn't have made it this far without them."

Meggy whinnied and tossed his head back as he nuzzled her hand for a sugar cube. "See, I told you you'd have the horses doing anything for you. And here he is getting ready to run in the biggest race of the year."

"Well, don't get too excited yet. We are in the mutuel field."

"What does that mean?"

Betsy rolled her eyes. "It means two things. One, it

means they haven't updated their betting machines. They can only take bets on a limited number of horses. And two, a committee picks which horses they think are the best and those are the ones you can bet individually on. The last extra horses are placed in the mutuel field and you bet on them as a group."

"But Meggy has been doing so well," Marcy said as she worried about placing all her savings on a group of horses the committee had basically lumped together as the losers.

"It's because I'm a woman. I can't tell you how much I've had to listen to them patronizing me. It took Beauford helping me to even get a reputable trainer. It's enough to make a feminist out of me," Betsy joked. "But I have faith in Meggy. He'll do great."

The band played "My Old Kentucky Home" and Marcy sang along with the other 123,000 racing fans in attendance. Marcy felt foolish as silent tears fell from her eyes as she sang, "Weep no more my lady. Oh weep no more today; we will sing one song for My Old Kentucky Home. For My Old Kentucky Home, far away."

Betsy squeezed her hand and she didn't have to tell her best friend that she was thinking of Jake so far away from his old Kentucky home. The song ended, the crowd cheered, and Marcy gripped Betsy's hand as the field of twenty horses entered the starting gate.

The bell sounded and the race was on. The horses in the mutuel field fell to the back of the race. Marcy groaned and closed her eyes. This was going to be the longest two minutes of her life.

"It's a battle for the lead as they hit the first quarter in twenty-three seconds," the announcer said excitedly.

Marcy had her hand over her eyes. "Where's Meggy?"

"Er," Betsy mumbled. Marcy had to strain to hear her friend over the announcer. "Sixteenth."

"Sixteenth!"

"Wait! Fifteenth!" Betsy tightened her grip. "Fourteenth. They just hit the half-mile mark and he's gaining on the outside. Go, Meggy! Come on, baby!"

Marcy moved her fingers so she could sneak a peek through them and sure enough, My Megavolt was on the move. "My Megavolt is thundering along the outside as they make the final turn at the three-quarters mark, but wait, here comes Courtier."

Marcy gave up trying to hide her eyes and joined in with the crowd as they cheered on their horses. "He's gaining! Oh my gosh, come on, Meggy!"

"Courtier blows through the field to take the lead!" the announcer screamed.

"Oh no, he's pulling away and Meggy is in fourth! Come on, Meggy!" Marcy screamed with desperation. All her money rode on this race as Courtier's lead grew and Meggy struggled to hold onto fourth. Marcy's stomach dropped when Courtier crossed the finish line first.

Betsy's head fell back as she laughed. Her beautiful red rose-themed hat bounced as she just laughed harder.

"I don't see how losing all our money is funny," Marcy snapped.

"But you don't know who Courtier is, do you?" Betsy said as she gasped for air.

"He's the one who cost me my savings," Marcy mumbled. She should never have bet more than she could have afforded to lose.

"He's the longest shot in the field and he just won the Derby. He was in the mutuel field with Meggy. Remember, we couldn't bet on Meggy individually, so we had to bet on the whole mutuel field."

Marcy blinked. The pieces were fitting together. "We won anyway!" Marcy fell into her seat with relief. Never again would she bet on anything.

The scoreboard flickered as the official results were posted and Betsy screamed, "We won almost two thousand dollars!"

Marcy practically fainted upon hearing Betsy.

Chapter Eight

J ake tore into the mail he had just received. Marcy wrote
  him a letter for every day of the month. Some soldiers
could be patient and read one a day, but not him. He read
them all and then re-read one at a time each day. Her first
letter was dated over a month ago telling him she sold some
alfalfa for a pretty good price. Apparently his wife was a
pretty good negotiator.

Beauford and Tabby had written him as well, telling
him they were helping Marcy run the farm, but she needed
them less and less. She had taken to farm life like a duck to
water. His chest filled with pride. He couldn't wait to brag
to the guys about how amazing his wife was.

By the tenth letter, he dropped it to the ground and
laughed until tears threatened to spill. It had taken her a
couple of days, but she'd finally told him she gambled with
her savings and ended up winning on a fluke. When he
picked up the letter, she surprised him further by telling
him she put half into savings and half into the farm. She'd
gotten a loan for some new equipment and was clearing
even more fields in the back of the property. Gone was the
young high school graduate he had left behind almost
eighteen months ago, and in her place was a resilient
woman.

He opened the next letter and read how Bertha, a pig

Tabby had given her, was almost fifty pounds now. She also read how Violet kept eyeing the poor animal for the breakfast menu. Soon he was laughing again as Marcy recounted a story about one of the high school seniors taking a bet to pinch Violet's behind. He ended up with a spatula to the face. It left a mark for almost a week.

His mood lifted as he tore into the twentieth letter. The crops were growing, the cows were fat, and the new tractor was a dream. Betsy had even ridden it in a sundress and pearls. Inside, he found a picture Betsy had taken of Marcy standing next to the tractor with a huge pig at her feet. His heart clutched with the pain of missing his beautiful wife as he looked down at her smiling face. She'd changed some. Her hair was longer, her breasts a little fuller, and her hips a little rounder. But her body was trimmer from all the hard work on the farm. She glowed with a tan, and some freckles had appeared on the bridge of her nose. And she had worn a miniskirt in the photo just for him. He picked the letter back up and continued to read.

> *I broke my promise. I had sworn I would never bet again, but I did. I made a five-dollar bet with the Rose sisters. See, Lily Rae had been vexed with John about how he found out the governor was coming to visit Keeneston before she did. Daisy was taking Mr. and Mrs. Wyatt's order when Mrs. Wyatt told them that she knew a secret about the reason for the governor's visit. Well, Lily Rae overheard and told them that she'd bet five dollars that she could find out the secret before John. And so it began. Daisy took the bets and Violet collected the money. After seeing what John has done to keep us connected, I hated to do it, but I bet against Lily. The good news — I won!*
>
> *John came rushing into the diner two days later and announced, much to Lily's dismay, that the governor*

BLUEGRASS DAWN

*was here to honor the Keeneston Ladies for the array of
volunteer work they do. He was naming May 30th
Keeneston Ladies' Day. Needless to say, Lily was not
pleased. She's now challenged John to a bet of picking the
day Tabby's sow will give birth. I'm not placing a bet on
that one.*

Jake chuckled as he read the rest of the letter. The
explosion ended what would have been a great day. The
letters dropped to the ground and were trampled into the
mud as all hell broke loose.

Marcy's small radio was attached to her tractor with an old
belt. It played Carole King's "I Feel the Earth Move" as she
worked in the fields. The sun was beating down on her, but
she didn't care. She sang for all the plants and cows as she
worked. She'd never thought that she would enjoy this type
of life, but the truth was she had never felt so fulfilled. If
only Jake was here with her, then her life would be perfect.

She looked at the sweet corn swaying in the light breeze
and sang louder for it. She'd planted those crops. She's
helped them grow and now she had full fields. She stopped
singing and tilted her head. Had she just heard something?

Looking around, she saw off in the far distance
something shiny and then she heard it again. She turned off
her tractor and put her hand across her brow to shield the
sun. The sheriff was speeding along with lights flashing.
His cruiser was sending up a dust cloud that only partially
hid Betsy's Mustang, Lily's Volkswagen Beetle, and John's
Mercury Cougar close behind.

The sheriff's cruiser slid to a stop in the field. Lily was

close behind. Marcy watched wide-eyed as Violet and Lily leapt from the front seat and Daisy struggled to climb from the super-tiny space in the back. But it was the two men who stepped out of the cruiser and the one that remained inside that drew her attention away from the Roses' car.

A member of the Army in dress uniform, followed by Father James, walked toward her as her friends scrambled from the cars.

"Good afternoon, ma'am. I'm Officer Whitlow with the Army." Marcy didn't even realize she'd climbed down from the tractor. "I have news about your husband, Second Lieutenant Davies."

Marcy felt foolish as *Oh, he got his promotion* ran through her head. She knew what was coming. She'd seen too many of these notifications to not know. She felt dead inside as she willed herself to remain standing.

"Your husband's unit was attacked. During the attack, your husband saved the life of his commanding officer and most of his unit. He tossed a grenade and took out a machine gun, giving his unit time to launch a counterattack. In the process, he was wounded."

Marcy didn't hear the gasps from everyone clustered behind the officer. She only gave a small nod to let him know she heard him. Her husband had died a hero. She wasn't surprised. He'd always been her hero.

"He was shot in the leg and is listed as seriously injured."

Marcy stopped mid-nod. "Injured? He's not dead?"

"No, ma'am. As I said, your husband was wounded saving the life of his commanding officer and many in his unit. He's being awarded the Purple Heart and probably more commendations. He is at a field hospital. He'll be fine, but his injury is severe enough to send him home once he's stable."

"He's coming home? Alive?" Marcy gasped.

"Yes, ma'am," the officer said with a large smile.

Marcy ignored the tears in her eyes and leapt onto the officer. She wrapped her arms around him and hugged him for all she was worth. "I thought . . ."

"Unfortunately, many people think that. We're not always the bad guys. We're commissioned to notify the family of any reason the soldier is unable to serve in the Army. It could be from illness, missing in action, injury, and so on. Not just death. I'll be returning to give you updates as I get them."

"When is he coming home?" Marcy asked as her friends surrounded her.

"I don't know yet. I'll be out here as soon as I find out. Have a good day, Mrs. Davies. And here is my card. Call me if you need anything."

"Thank you!" Marcy grabbed the card and held it tightly in her hand. Her husband was coming home alive.

The officer got back in the car with the sheriff and Father James who had a smile so wide she could hardly see his eyes. Today was a happy day. Today, the earth had fallen from beneath her feet but had been rebuilt stronger.

"We have to plan a party," Lily said as she wiped tears of joy from her eyes. "John, work your magic and find out when our boy is coming home."

"Yes, ma'am!" John saluted happily before picking Marcy up and swinging her around in celebration.

Marcy laughed and shook her head. "Should we be celebrating that Jake was shot?"

"We're celebrating his life and the fact that he saved others. Helen would be so proud. I'll put flowers on her grave on the way home for all of us tonight," Daisy sniffled.

"What are his favorite foods?" Violet asked. "Make a list and bring it to work tonight. We'll share the news with the whole town — that is, if John hasn't already."

After hugs and happy tears, the Rose sisters crammed back into the Beetle and tore out for town. Marcy turned to Betsy and confessed.

"I'm so excited. But Betsy, what do I do?"

"What do you mean?"

"I'm not the same person I was eighteen months ago. And I'm sure he's not either. What if we don't love each other the same anymore?" Marcy had never thought about it before. She'd been too worried about Jake coming home alive to worry about it, but now he was coming home. "What if he's disappointed in the farm? What if he no longer finds me attractive? What if . . ."

"Marcy!" Betsy laughed as she held up her hands. "I understand your fears. I do. But you're worrying too much. You have a love that runs deep. It doesn't just disappear. It simply forms a new bend as it winds through life. And those bends are the interesting parts."

Marcy let out a long breath. "You're right. I'm going to get a haircut. And I need to clean the house and bathe the pig."

"You do know it will be a while before he's home, right?"

"I don't care. It's going to be ready for whenever he gets here. I can't believe it; my husband's coming home!"

Chapter Nine

J ake's stomach was in knots as the Kentucky Air
National Guard plane landed at the Bluegrass Airport.
He had flown into Travis Air Force Base in California but
had talked his way onto the Guard plane instead of having
to fly commercial from San Francisco. He guessed that was
a perk of saving a high-ranking officer.

His leg was still sore, but he was able to walk with only
a slight limp after a month of recovery and had been
assured that physical therapy should eventually remove the
limp. Would Marcy think of him as less of a man? Would
the jagged scar on his thigh scare her? What would she
think of him after all this time away? Would she still want
him?

The plane slowed and taxied down the runway on the
far side of the airport away from the civilian planes. Aboard
the cargo plane were the pilots and flag-draped coffins of
Kentucky soldiers who had given their lives for their
country.

Jake had spent the long, uncomfortable flight in agony.
He couldn't wait to get home, but he was nervous at the
same time. How much had changed since he had left? It felt
like a lifetime. The co-pilot peered around the door to
where he sat in the cargo area. "You think all these people
are here for you?"

"What?" Jake asked as he was pulled from his worrying.

"Come up here and have a look."

Jake stood and walked stiffly into the small cockpit. He leaned over the instruments and looked out the small window. "Welcome Home" banners were hung on the chain link fence. Half the town of Keeneston stood waving flags and signs behind the fence. And right in front was Marcy jumping up and down and waving her hands in the air.

Marcy clung to the fence as she watched the large cargo plane slow to a stop. With a wink and a good show of cleavage, Violet had talked a man working in the nearby hangar to open the gate after the plane arrived. It seemed like forever as the huge plane finally shut down its engines and the man opened the gate for them.

Marcy ran. She didn't hear the clapping and cheering from the townspeople. She didn't hear the other planes landing on the runways on the other side of the airport. She didn't hear anything except her excited breathing as she sprinted forward.

And then the back ramp of the plane opened and there Jake stood. He was in dress uniform and hurrying down the ramp as fast as he could with the cane. Marcy's steps faltered. She had known Jake had been injured, but it was different seeing it. He was different. She saw it in an instant. His normally thick muscular body was now lean. She had a sudden desire to feed him. His strides were strong, but she could see the slight grimace on his now angular face when he put weight on his injured leg. Would he be different? Would he remember her? But then he looked up and saw her. Their eyes connected and all her worries fell away.

Jake smiled at her and held out his arms. Marcy broke out in tears and flung herself into his arms. She wrapped her legs around his waist and grabbed his shoulders with her arms. Jake stumbled back as he took her impact. She didn't hear his cane drop to the ground as he wrapped his arms around her in return. He still smelled like Jake. Even if he hadn't been to the farm in more than eighteen months, he still smelled like the country air. And his arms were just as she remembered. She still fit perfectly against his chest as they clung to each other.

"Is this real? Are you really here?" Marcy asked into his neck.

"It feels like heaven. I've been waiting a lifetime for this." Jake leaned back to look at her face. "You're even more beautiful than in my dreams."

Marcy smiled at him. His hazel eyes seemed more mature now, but they still sparkled with a hint of mischief as he bent his head to hers. His lips brushed hers softly, as if testing her to see if she was, in fact, real. Then Marcy threw caution to the wind and kissed him for all she was worth. Her husband was finally home.

Their reunion lasted as long as it took for the rest of the town to catch up to them. The Rose sisters all hugged Jake and gave joyful looks to Marcy. They had made it. As a town, they had stuck together and were celebrating one of their own making his way back home. Soon the Roses drifted to where the pilots had joined in the celebration. Lily and Violet batted their lashes and tossed their long straight hair over their shoulders. Daisy stood by and smiled blankly. Daisy's love was still overseas, or at least that's all she'd say about it. While Lily and Violet had no problem flirting, Daisy took more of an observational role. Marcy had always been curious about Daisy and Robert but right now they were the furthest things from her mind.

Betsy excitedly filled Jake in on how great Marcy has been on the farm. She joked that he would hardly know her, and Jake's face froze at the same time Marcy's did. It was the truth. They had been apart as much as they had been together. But then he smiled and squeezed her hand and she knew they'd work it out. It might take some time to remember why they fell in love, but those seeds were planted deep. She knew they'd make it. It might take some work, but their love was worth it.

Tabby whooped and hollered his welcome home as he thumped Jake on the back and sent Marcy a wink. Reverend Hamilton and Father James praised God while the Keeneston Belles and Keeneston Ladies all vowed to help Marcy put some weight back on him. Marcy clung to Jake as the single women made a fuss over him. The fact was she wasn't used to being married and was a little self-conscious about it.

"I'd appreciate that, ladies, but first I've been dreaming about my wife's fried chicken and brownies for almost two years." Jake's eyes sparkled and his lips stretched into a roguish grin. "And a few other things involving my wife."

The girls twittered at the comment, but Marcy didn't notice. Jake had kissed her again. Only Father James clearing his throat stopped them from progressing further right there on the runway.

"We have a big celebration planned for tonight at the café. Y'all go home and spend some time together and we'll see you later," Daisy instructed as she tried to round the town up.

"Okay," Marcy and Jake said at the same time, never taking their eyes away from one another.

Jake grabbed her hand and looked around once they

were alone. "Where's the truck?"

"Over there," Marcy pointed and Jake grabbed her hand as they hurried for his old truck.

He tossed his bag in the back and opened the door for Marcy. He noticed she was about to go to the driver's door, but he had plans for them. He backed her up against the truck and kissed her deeply. God, he'd missed her. He ran his hands roughly up her body and when she moaned into his mouth, he almost forgot about his plans.

Jake helped Marcy into the truck and hurried as fast as he could—curse his leg—to get into the truck. He tore out of the airport and toward Parkers Mill Road as fast as he could. Jake was having the hardest time staying on the road. He wanted to keep his eyes on Marcy to drink in every detail. Plus, it was foolish, but he was afraid he'd blink and he'd be back in Vietnam alone in his tent.

"Where are we going?" Marcy asked him as he pulled off the road a short time later in Keeneston.

"To the place that means the most to me."

He could see when Marcy figured out where he was heading. It was closer than his home and it was where his life changed forever. The pond came into view as the truck bounced along the dirt road.

"Why, I don't have my bathing suit," Marcy said in mock innocence.

"What a shame. Whatever will we do?"

The Rose sisters looked at the clock hanging on the wall of the café. Jake and Marcy should have been here an hour ago.

"I bet you five dollars there will be a baby within the year," Lily said as the café erupted into unabashed betting.

Chapter Ten

Jake put his hands behind his head and looked up at the bright blue sky. He'd only been home for a day and already the tension of the war was starting to fade. As he held Marcy in their bed the night before, he'd only had one bad dream. He didn't even cry out in his sleep as he had in the hospital. Keeneston soothed his soul and Marcy was the best nurse he could ask for.

The night before, they'd finally made it to the café with wet hair and smiles that wouldn't leave their faces. They stayed only long enough to eat and then raced back home. They'd made it as far as the driveway—as soon as he parked the truck, in fact. Twenty minutes later he walked into his house for the first time.

Marcy had changed the house enough to make it hers, but he still felt touches left behind from his mother. It was strange walking into the silent house, but he felt at peace with it. Tabby, Father James, Sheriff Mulford, and Marcy had written in such detail about the events leading up to his mother's death that he felt as if he had been there. He had grieved half a world away and had found peace with it.

When he had looked at Marcy standing in the middle of the living room with her clothes held together by her hands and her hair a tangled mess, he knew the grieving period was over. He'd miss his mother just as he missed his father, but his future was standing right in front of him. Someday children would fill that house and he knew that would please his parents more than anything.

A cloud passed overhead and Marcy rolled off him onto the fresh-cut grass. She didn't bother covering herself. They were in a newly cleared backfield and were miles from the road.

Jake turned his head and smiled at her. "Thanks for the tour of the property. You're absolutely amazing. Delivering cows, clearing fields . . . you made the property even more prosperous than I ever could. And here I was worried you wouldn't know what to do."

Jake pulled her close to him and ran his hand over her hair as she laid her head on his chest. "I wouldn't have been able to do it without our friends. Tabby and Betsy were a huge help. And the boys from the high school helped with the harvest so I was able to get more out of it."

"I'm so proud of you, Marcy," Jake told her before kissing the top of her head. "You are an amazing woman."

"I've missed you so much."

"I've missed you, too, sweetheart."

The silence of the field was disrupted by the squeal of a pig as Bertha pushed her way between them and lay down with a giant whoosh of air.

Jake just shook his head. "I can't believe you have a pet pig."

Marcy laughed as Bertha snorted in the grass. "Don't blame me. You're the one who told Tabby to keep an eye on me. You know how he loves his pigs. I'm just flattered he trusted me enough with one of them."

"Well, come on, Bertha. Let's see the rest of the farm and hear what my wife has planned for it."

"What *we* have planned for it. It's almost time for the fall harvest and I can't wait to get your opinions for what to do with some of the land for next year."

Marcy jumped up and stepped into her jeans. She'd been nervous about showing Jake what she had done. But with every word of praise he gave her, her confidence was bolstered. Soon she was dragging him over acres and acres of land, pointing out new things, telling him of new farm equipment, and working together to plot out their future.

Daisy Mae folded the letter and put it in the middle of *Little Women* before closing the thick book and putting it away forever. Her heart was broken. The life she had planned was not to be. Just as it had been with her sisters, she was destined to a life alone. At least she had her sisters and at least she had her café.

Violet Fae had taken her heartbreak and turned it into the Blossom Café. It was in her grief that she had come up with the idea. Lily Rae had taken her heartbreak in typical Lily fashion. She'd pushed it out of her mind and acted as if it had never happened. Only Daisy saw it when Lily flirted with other men. It was an act. A good act, but an act nonetheless. Daisy just didn't think she had it in her to give such a performance.

Daisy picked up the telephone and slowly turned the rotary until she heard ringing. "Violet. It's over."

"I'll be right over and I'll bring Lily with me."

Daisy nodded into the phone and hung up. She had her sisters, her café, and her town. They would be enough. She'd never let another person she cared about suffer a broken heart like she felt. No, she'd help them find love.

Daisy walked through her small cottage house and took down the pictures of Robert. She found an old box and gently laid them in it. She couldn't bear to throw them away, but she couldn't look at them either. She'd been happy once, and she'd be happy again.

Her sister didn't bother knocking. The front door burst open and Violet came in with a pitcher of lemonade and a pitcher of ice tea. "I thought we could make some Arnold Palmers."

Daisy gave a pained smile. "Thanks. Sounds wonderful." Just smiling hurt. She wanted to forget the pain, just for a night.

"I'm here!" Lily called as she burst into the small house. "What did I miss? Are you okay?"

"Vi brought Arnold Palmers and we were just going to sit down. I want you two to make me forget everything for one night."

Lily gave a big grin. "I can do that." She held up a fifth of bourbon and shook it temptingly.

The three sisters looked at the bourbon and over to where Violet Fae was mixing the lemonade and iced tea. With a mischievous grin, Lily hurried over and poured the bourbon in the mix.

Violet mixed the concoction and Lily poured it into the glasses. The sisters lifted the glasses and eyed them suspiciously.

"To my sisters," Daisy toasted.

"To love. Whenever, whoever, and however it comes to be," Violet toasted.

"To Keeneston. A place we can always love," Lily toasted. They all looked at each other nervously. "Bottoms up!"

Daisy and her sisters lifted the glasses to their mouths

and took a deep drink. Daisy coughed and the girls giggled.

"That's good," Violet said, surprised.

"I think we can make it better. What do you have in the ice box and fridge, Daisy?" Lily asked as she was already heading for the kitchen.

Daisy giggled as the bourbon warmed her. Soon they were mixing limes, tea, and everything but the kitchen sink in their drink until somewhere around midnight they found the perfect recipe and Daisy forgot the pain she was in.

Chapter Eleven

M arcy heard the screen door open. She smiled as Jake
brought her a blanket to wrap around her flannel
nightgown as she looked out over the snowy fields. The
months had flown by now that they were together. Jake had
gone to the doctor once a week for therapy on his leg and
was now able to walk without a cane. He was on track to be
completely healed in just a few more months.

The infection that had riddled the injury while in the
jungle had slowed his recovery, but she knew he was
determined enough to work on it until his leg was healed.

"It's so peaceful in the mornings," Marcy told him as
she blew on her hot chocolate. "I love sitting out here. Even
the cold weather isn't going to stop me."

"It makes me think of peace. There's tranquility in it.
The sun cracking over the horizon, the red cardinals sitting
on the fences, the quiet sound of cows in the distance — it
centers me and gets me excited about the day. I can't wait to
get out there and work," Jake told her as he took a seat next
to her with his coffee.

"I'll help you feed the animals and check on things. But,
it's Christmas Eve and I want to bake some pies for the
town party out at the Wyatts' house."

"That's okay. I don't mind doing it myself. Especially if
that means you have time to make an extra pie just for us."

Jake grinned like a schoolboy getting a treat.

Marcy couldn't resist. "Anything for you." Suddenly she had a desire to call her mother. They hadn't talked in almost a year — since her birthday, in fact. Her brother had had twins and her mother was too busy with being a grandmother to talk long. But it was Christmas and Marcy was determined to talk to her family and let go of the bitterness she held for being constantly left out. Besides, she had her own family now. Jake and Keeneston never made her feel left out.

"I'm off. Come on, Bertha," Jake leaned over and gave his wife a kiss before standing up and heading for the barn with a big fat pink pig trailing happily after him.

Marcy went inside and changed clothes. She got out the flour and eggs and mixed the dough just as Helen had taught her. Today and tomorrow she was making all of the Davies family holiday recipes. It was their first Christmas together as husband and wife and she intended to make a big deal out of it. She'd been saving a few extra dollars every week and had bought Jake the perfect Christmas gift. She couldn't wait to give it to him. She'd put in so much thought and knew he'd love it.

Marcy hummed to herself as she mixed the dough and sliced the apples. Finally it was late enough that she could call her mother. She knew they'd be at Scott's house since his wife was now in charge of the family as the oldest wife.

Kevin was newly married but if she knew her mother, it was all about seniority. Marcy had received an invitation before she'd known about Jake's injury. She had written them and told them she was holding down the fort at home and wouldn't be able to make it.

She got nervous as the phone rang. She hadn't talked to her brothers for years.

"Merry Christmas!" a woman said happily over the phone. The sound of laughter and cheer in the background came through crystal clear and Marcy felt the familiar feeling of being on the outside looking in.

"Merry Christmas. You must be Debra. I'm Marcy Davies. Um, Faulkner."

"Oh! Scott's little sister. Far-out!"

"Marcy?" She heard Scott ask from the background. "What does she want? Is she okay?"

"I think so. She sounds fine," her sister-in-law said as she covered the phone with her hand. "Sorry. It's so nice to talk to you. With the cost of long distance, it's just so hard to call. And it's been crazy with Scott and Kevin just returning a couple months ago from their deployment. Thank goodness for Mom or I don't know what I would have done," Debra laughed.

Marcy felt horrible. The green monster of jealousy reared its head. Her mother hadn't bothered to help her while she ran a massive farm by herself, worrying every day that her new husband may be dead.

"Yeah. Well, I just wanted to wish you all a Merry Christmas."

"Wait! Scott wants to talk to you."

"Hey, sis!" Her brother actually sounded happy to hear from her.

"Hi, Scott. How are you? Mom said you were deployed?"

"No biggie. We were in the Mediterranean Sea mostly keeping an eye on things. What's going on with you? Did you hear I'm a father now? And guess what? Debra just found out she's expecting again."

"That's great. Jake and I don't have any kids yet. In fact, he just got back from Vietnam a couple months ago. We're taking our time and enjoying getting to know each other again." Marcy smiled to herself. Oh boy, were they enjoying it.

"You better hurry up. You're not getting any younger."

"I'm not even twenty yet. I think I have some time."

"Maybe if you just want one," Scott laughed. "Anyway, great to hear from you, sis. Too bad you didn't make it to Kevin's wedding. It was a huge shindig. Mom was crying all over the place with happiness. Dad was even dancing. Oh, here's Mom. Ma! It's Marcy," Scott told her as he handed off the phone.

"Are you trying to come home? I'm not sending you any money."

"What?" Marcy asked, confused.

Her mother sighed. "What do you want, Marcy?"

"It's Christmas. I thought I'd wish everyone a Merry Christmas and let you know how I'm doing."

"We have too much to do today to hear about that. Debra and Brenda—she's Kevin's wife—and myself have a lot of cooking to do."

"Well, Merry Christmas. Mom? Why don't you like me?"

"What nonsense are you talking about? See, I told you I don't have time for this. Your brothers are waiting. I'm making them their favorite pancakes. Good-bye."

Marcy held out the phone and stared at it. Her mother had hung up on her. She had known her brothers were the darlings of the family, but knowing she wasn't missed at all by her parents, and just a side thought to her brothers, crushed her.

She hung up the phone and picked up a rolling pin. She viciously worked out the dough until she had quit crying. She would take the high road and send a Christmas card every year. But if they wanted more than that, then it was up to them to make the move. She'd love them in her heart and that would be enough. As her mother said, that was a woman's lot and Marcy had decided to accept her lot in her family.

When she lifted her head, she saw Jake walking across the pasture holding a small calf with a pig and a huge mama cow trailing after him. Her heart swelled and a smile spread across her face. Jake turned toward the house and smiled at her. She had her own family now. And in a couple years, when she and Jake were ready, they would have kids of their own — a whole bunch of them. And she would raise them to love one another, not to compete to be the favorite.

Yes, she knew she'd do it because Helen had taught her how in that last year of her life. Helen had been the mother Marcy wanted to be some day.

Chapter Twelve

T he door to the Wyatts' stood wide open as people carried casserole dishes and platters into the huge historic house. Garlands framed the door and white lights lit up the yard from where they were hung on magnolia trees. Mrs. Wyatt stood by the front door in a long red velvet dress. Her face was powdered white and her lips matched her dress. A green hat sat jauntily on her head as she directed the people carrying in the food.

"Merry Christmas! Marcy, is that the famous Davies family apple pie I smell?" Mrs. Wyatt kissed her cheek and then kissed Jake, leaving a bright red lipstick imprint on his cheek.

Marcy smiled. The feeling of love from her Keeneston family made her forget the phone call from that morning. Sometimes things were just unexplainable and her mother's choice to love only her sons was one of them. But as the town greeted them with open arms, cheer and peace settled over her.

The house was filled with people talking and laughing. Every person had a bright red lipstick stain on their cheek but didn't seem to mind. In fact, it was a badge of honor.

"Jake!"

"William!" Jake hurried to shake his friend's hand. "I didn't know you were going to be here."

"I got three days of leave to celebrate Christmas." His arm was around Betsy and it looked like it would stay there all evening. "It's damn good to see you. How are you feeling?"

"Really good. I got rid of that cane and the leg is improving every day."

"I heard you'll be honored with the Purple Heart."

"I will. But for right now I'm just happy to be home alive with my wife."

Marcy hugged Betsy, which was pretty awkward considering William wasn't relinquishing his hold on her. Betsy just rolled her eyes and they both laughed. It was a shared laugh of happiness and friendship. They had been through so much together and now they were able to celebrate. Relief and joy filled the house as Marcy made her way to the kitchen to put the pies on the dessert table.

The Rose sisters were all wearing matching mini dresses, tights, and knee-high boots. Their long hair was decorated with different-colored headbands and they were clustered around a punch bowl. Lily was pouring something into it as Violet stirred and Daisy kept a lookout.

When Daisy saw her, she nudged Lily and then spoke loudly. "Why, Marcy, you look lovely tonight."

Marcy narrowed her eyes and walked over to them. "Okay, what are you three up to?"

"Nothing," Lily Rae said innocently. Lily was never innocent.

"Now I know you're hiding something."

Violet smiled sweetly and handed her a glass of punch. "Here, have some punch."

Marcy set her pies down and took the cup. She looked at it suspiciously before taking a tentative sip. She coughed as the liquid burned as it went down.

Violet frowned. "Too much bourbon. Daisy, pour in a cup of limeade and I think it will be good."

"You're spiking the punch?" Marcy asked as she grinned in wonder. What wouldn't these sisters do?

"Don't tell Reverend Hamilton," Daisy whispered as the young clergyman strode into the kitchen.

"Punch, Reverend?" Lily asked sweetly.

The reverend took the punch and sipped it. "Hmm, thank you." He took a cookie off a platter and ambled back out.

Lily looked at them and grinned evilly. "He'll be snockered after one glass."

"I can't believe you're getting the reverend drunk," Marcy hissed as she tried not to laugh.

"Then he shouldn't have snipped off a couple of my prize-winning rosebuds this summer. He snuck over in the middle of the night. Bless his heart, but did he think I wouldn't catch him?"

Marcy just shook her head and took another glass of punch. "Your secret is safe with me."

As she headed into the two large rooms at the front of the house, she heard John Wolfe before she saw him.

"Ho-ho-ho, Merry Christmas!" John was dressed as Santa Claus and his wife was dressed as Mrs. Claus. "Has everyone been good little boys and girls?"

Everyone laughed and clamored around John as he handed out little jars of his local, pure honey. It was good enough that Marcy would elbow her way through the crowd, friends be damned.

"I got one, Marcy! No need to take out Tom's knees this year. He needs them to get back to studying at law school," Jake teased.

"Ha-ha. You know that was an accident."

"Marcy," a voice said softly from behind her. Marcy turned and saw Linda Miller. They had been friends in high school. She had married an avid fisherman from their class named Merlin and moved to the coast so he could get a job on a boat in Massachusetts.

"Linda! I didn't you were back."

"We just got back this week. We bought a house out in the country. Merlin made good money on the boats, but we missed home. And with me being pregnant and all, we thought we would move back."

"You're pregnant? I can't even tell." Marcy looked at Linda's still-flat stomach in wonder.

"I'm just ten weeks along."

"Congratulations!" Marcy said excitedly. She noticed everyone started looking at her stomach. Did the sweater dress she was wearing make her look fat? She didn't know why else everyone would be looking at her tummy.

"What about you? What have you been doing since we graduated?"

"Helping Jake run the farm. He was in Vietnam. He came home this summer after being injured. But we're good now. No plans for kids yet. We are just enjoying being with each other for a bit."

Marcy looked up again when the people around her groaned.

"Do you have names picked out yet?" Marcy asked absently as she looked at the people all whispering with sad looks on their faces.

"Oh yes. I was so excited I had them already picked out. Eugenia if it's a girl or Eugene if it's a boy," Linda said as she absently set her hand to her stomach.

"Oh!" Marcy said, not really knowing how to respond politely. "Well, bless his or her little heart. I look forward to seeing you around town. Let's get together for dinner soon."

"Sounds great. Merry Christmas," Linda said as she smiled before heading to say hi to some of the Belles from her class. Unfortunately, by marrying Merlin, she was iffy on her Belle membership. Upon marrying a man of good "breeding" and "status," a Belle became a Keeneston Lady. And Merlin wasn't considered to have either breeding or status. He was the nicest man, but he was poor, smelled perpetually like fish, and didn't give a fig about social standing. Marcy loved him — the Belles, not so much.

"How ya doing, Jake?" Beauford asked in his easygoing Southern way. His voice was deep and he spoke slowly. But don't let that fool you, he was a financial genius. He also had a passion for three-piece suits, which he wore every day. The farming and horse racing were really Mrs. Wyatt's thing.

"I'm doing well, sir. Thank you for having us at your house tonight."

Beauford laughed and slapped his shoulder. "Of course, son! My sweetpea wouldn't have it any other way. And since you're a married man now, I'm sure you've discovered that a happy wife is a happy life."

Jake grinned. He *had* discovered that. And he liked now being in this married men's club. All the older men in town seemed to want to talk to him tonight. He was being asked his opinion on politics, local projects, and farming. And when Marcy came up to him and handed him a glass of punch, he felt completely at ease with his new life. He was ready to make these big decisions and be part of the conversation. He wanted to help the town that supported him and make a better future for the children he hoped to have one day. So when he was asked if he would run for the town council, he said he'd think about it. And he meant it.

Marcy slid her arm around his waist and listened as he talked town politics. Her support gave him the strength to step out on his own. He'd always been his parents' son, but now he was the head of the Davies family. His chest filled with pride and warmth as he drank another glass of punch.

Marcy continued to smile up at him as she handed him another glass. He rolled up his sleeves. Was it hot in here? It had to be with so many people. Was that his wife's hand on his bottom? He looked down at her as he talked to the mayor and saw her paying attention to what the man was saying, but then he felt the squeeze and knew it had to be her.

Jake cleared his throat. "That's fascinating, Mr. Mayor. I'll think on that. Excuse me for a moment. My wife has something she's been wanting to show me."

Marcy batted her eyelashes innocently at him and politely excused them from their conversation. Jake dragged her through the room and out the kitchen door. He ignored the looks the Rose sisters sent him and the way Father James crossed himself.

"My sweet, innocent wife isn't so innocent, is she?" he whispered as he pulled her into the nearest barn.

"Who, me?"

Jake sat down on a bale of hay and pulled her onto his lap. "I think you've got a naughty side and that's just fine by me," Jake kissed her then and Marcy shoved her hands under his suit coat to feel his chest.

"As long as there is a breath left in my body, I'm going to want to do this with you," he murmured as he kissed his way down her neck.

"I would worry about what the people at the party would think, but I want you too much to care."

And when Marcy undid his zipper, the last thing he was thinking about was the party.

The Roses stood with Father James staring at the door that had just slammed shut behind the smoldering Jake and Marcy.

"Go forth and be fruitful," Father James said before making the sign of the cross in the air.

"I have five bucks that says this time she'll be pregnant with a babe in her arms in nine months," Lily said as she handed Father James a glass of punch.

"I'll go in on that," he replied as he dug out five dollars.

Chapter Thirteen

Marcy woke up with a start. It was Christmas! She pried Jake's hand from her bare breast and rolled quietly out of bed. She slipped on her robe and hurried downstairs to start breakfast and Jake's coffee. By the time the bacon was done frying, Jake was already in his robe and coming down the stairs.

"Merry Christmas, sweetheart," Jake said as he planted a lingering kiss on her lips. His hands slipped into her robe and Marcy sighed with pleasure. If she could start the morning like this everyday, then she'd be a happy woman.

"Merry Christmas. Breakfast is ready. I can't wait for you to open my gift!" Marcy said excitedly. She'd thought about it for months and saved up for it. It was the perfect gift.

"Me, too," Jake said as he bit into a piece of bacon.

"Okay, breakfast can wait!" Marcy laughed as she dragged Jake out of the chair and into the living room. They had a small tree set up in the corner with some of the Davies family bulbs on it. Underneath it were presents from the Rose sisters, Betsy and William, the one from Jake, and the ones Marcy had gotten for him.

They opened the gifts from their friends first and laughed as Lily sent them baby booties, Daisy sent them a baby blanket, and Violet sent them a baby bonnet. "I think they may be trying to tell us something."

"Too bad they have to wait for us to use them," Jake shook his head as he laughed. "I'm not ready to share you yet."

"Me neither. In three years, well, that's another story. I'll probably be sick of you by then," Marcy joked.

Jake leaned over from where they sat on the floor and kissed her deeply. "Are you sure about that?"

"Keep that up and I'll never want to share you. Here, open the gift from William and Betsy."

Jake ripped into it and Marcy gasped. It was an oil painting of their farm. It showed green rolling hills dotted with cows and a white farmhouse with two people holding hands as they stood on the porch looking out at the land.

"It's beautiful," Marcy said softly as she ran her hand over it. "I had wondered why Betsy would sit in her car in front of our house for so long when she came to visit."

She would have to thank her friend for such a heartfelt gift. It would hang in their house forever. Marcy stood and walked over to the living room wall. She took down a decorative mirror and hung up the painting, smiling as she looked at it.

"Now it's time for your gift!" Marcy said as she turned around. She pulled out the big box and pushed it to him.

Jake tore into the paper. "A record player! Oh, this is great, Marcy. You know how much I love music. Thank you so much."

Marcy couldn't stop grinning. "And don't forget this." She handed him a big square box. She couldn't contain her excitement. She knew he'd love it.

He opened the box and stared at the records. "Led Zeppelin, Rolling Stones, Johnny Cash, Waylon Jennings, and Merle Haggard. Wow," he said in awe. "Dolly Parton?"

Marcy shrugged her shoulders. "That one is for me. Do you like it?"

"Like it? I love it! I can't believe you got all my favorite records. How did you afford a record player?"

"I worked at the café at night to save up money while you were gone. I knew how much you liked music and thought you could take it out to the barn while you worked and that we could dance in the living room at night."

Jake leapt up and wrapped her in a tight hug. "I love it. It's the best gift I've ever gotten. Here, open mine."

Jake handed Marcy the heavy rectangular box. Marcy smiled giddily at him and slid her finger under the tape and slowly unwrapped it. He knew she would love it. Every couple of days since he got back, he'd heard her complaining about her old one.

"A new iron?" she asked slowly as she pulled it out of the box.

"That's right. So you don't have to complain about the old one. I know it was giving you . . ."

Thunk.

Jake batted his eyes and rubbed his head. Did his wife just hit him in the head with her Christmas gift?

"You got me an iron for our first Christmas? An iron!"

"But, you hated the old one."

"It's an iron, Jake!"

Jake rubbed his head again. "It's an expensive, top-of-the-line iron," he said defensively.

"Good! Then you can use it when you iron your clothes."

"Me? I don't know how to iron clothes. That's not fun."

"No kidding! Do you think I enjoy doing it?"

"Well, I don't know."

"Men!" Marcy threw up her arms and stomped from the room.

"Does this mean I don't get any apple pie tonight?"

Marcy pushed open the swinging door and glared at him. "You won't be getting apple pie from me for a very long time, Jake Davies!"

The door swung shut and Jake was left sitting on the floor with an iron by his feet, a bump on his head, and an angry wife in the kitchen. Where had he gone wrong?

"You got her an iron? For your first Christmas together?" Beauford Wyatt drawled.

"Yes," Jake whispered into the phone. He didn't know whom else to call. Beauford had been good friends with his father and had been married for a while. If anyone could help him, it was Beauford.

Jake could hear him trying not to laugh. "Son, that was quite possibly the stupidest thing you could have done."

"But . . ."

"No buts about it. You don't give your wife a gift like that for Christmas or her birthday. That's a random day kind of thing. And it's never a gift. It's like, 'Oh, I picked this up today' type thing. Christmas needs to be romantic and thoughtful. While you put some thought into the iron, it wasn't *thoughtful*. You basically told her you appreciate her as a maid."

"Oh," Jake frowned. "I didn't think about it like that. What do I do now?"

"You need a Christmas miracle, son."

Jake hung up the phone and sat quietly on the couch. What was he going to do? He'd messed up big time. Thoughtful. Romantic. Oh boy. He was in trouble. Jake got up and started pacing. He heard Marcy banging pots and pans around in the kitchen and decided it would be wise if he stayed out of there for now.

Romantic. The only romantic thing they'd done together was stay at the bed-and-breakfast. Wait! They'd never had a honeymoon! But, how was he going to pull that off on Christmas day?

Jake reached for the phone again. If anyone could help it, it was Santa.

Marcy slammed the pot onto the stove and grumbled. "Stupid, stupid man. Who does he think I am? The little lady of the house who can't wait to iron his stupid boxers?"

She turned on the stove and reached for the cast-iron skillet to make some rolls. "I'm just the little lady of the house making Christmas dinner."

There was a soft knock on the kitchen door and she turned with the skillet still in hand. Jake's head slowly appeared. When she didn't bash him with the heavy pan, he stepped the rest of the way into the kitchen. Marcy's breath caught as she saw the two suitcases he set down.

"You're leaving me?" she gasped.

"*We're* leaving. Turn off the stove." Jake walked slowly into the kitchen and hesitantly reached for the skillet. He took it from her hands and put it away.

Marcy just stood there as he wrapped up food and put it in the freezer. He dumped the pot of water, dried it, and put it away. "What's going on?"

Jake locked the door and turned off the kitchen lights. He took her hand in his and led her from the room. He stopped only to pick up the suitcases. "Go get dressed, Marcy."

"Not until you tell me what's going on."

"That would ruin my apology. Now, go get dressed."

Marcy took a deep breath. An apology was good. "Fine." She hurried up the stairs and pulled out some slacks and a blouse. Maybe he was taking her to a romantic day out and then to dinner at a fancy restaurant, but that wouldn't explain the suitcases.

She hurried back downstairs. "I'm ready. Where are we going?"

"It's a surprise."

Jake locked the door behind them and escorted her to the truck. Maybe a night at the bed-and-breakfast. But then they drove passed it and toward Lexington. Oh! Maybe a night at one of the fancy hotels downtown. But, then he turned before they got to downtown.

"The airport?" Marcy guessed as they turned onto Parkers Mill Road.

"You'll just have to see."

Jake parked the car and Marcy started feeling giddy. This was so exciting. Where were they going? She'd never been on a plane before.

Jake led her into the small Bluegrass Airport terminal and set her on a plastic chair. "Wait here."

She watched as he went to the ticket counter and then came back with two tickets. "Where are we going?" Marcy asked with unabashed giddiness.

"Nowhere until you forgive me. I'm so sorry I was such a dunce. This is our first Christmas together and you put so much thought into your present and I just got the first thing I heard you say you wanted. It didn't occur to me that it's not a very romantic gift. I know you're not my maid and to prove it, will you please teach me to iron?"

Marcy laughed and shook her head. "Yes, I'll teach you to iron. With pleasure!"

"Since I'm on a roll, will you forgive me for being such

a nincompoop?"

"Yes, I'll forgive you. It seems you've more than made up for it. *Now,* will you tell me where we are going?"

"Nope," Jake grinned and her knees turned wobbly.

Jake held out his hand and they walked through the terminal. She passed each gate wondering if this was the one they would be going to. So many places all over the world were at the tip of her fingers.

"Now boarding for Fort Lauderdale," a gate attendant said into the loudspeaker.

"Are we going there?" Marcy asked with barely contained excitement as they approached the gate where the stewardess was dressed as a cute Mrs. Claus.

"Yes, it is," Jake said with a worried smile. "Is it okay?"

"I love you!" Marcy yelled as she jumped onto him. Jake caught her and laughed as she squealed with delight.

The stewardess smiled at them and took the tickets from Jake.

"I've never been to the beach. I can't believe it. You can get me household appliances anytime if this is how you make up for it. I can't wait to swim in the ocean," Marcy said as she dragged Jake toward the plane.

"Unfortunately, they require bathing suits at the ocean," Jake said with a dramatic sigh.

"Don't worry, I'll find a way to make that up to you," Marcy whispered as they boarded the plane.

"Maybe I will get you a mixer for our anniversary if this is what I get when I do something to make up for it," Jake grinned.

"Jake Davies! You better not get me a mixer!"

"Don't worry. I've learned my lesson and you have a lifetime of reminding me I got you an iron."

"We learn something new about each other every day.

It makes marriage exciting," Marcy said as she took her seat by the window.

The stewardess brought over some chocolate and champagne for the few people flying on Christmas day.

Jake raised his glass. "To our marriage. May we love each other a little more every year."

"And may we take the ups and the downs in stride, always growing closer as we do."

"And to the beginning of many Christmases together. They may change as we add children to our family, but I will always remember you in that robe, the iron, and the best make-up sex we'll ever have."

"Well, cheers to that," Marcy quipped as they clicked glasses and flew toward their future.

Epilogue

Marcy looked over the dining room table to where Jake sat at the other end. His shoulders were still broad. He still wore flannel shirts with worn blue jeans. His cowboy hat still hung on the peg by the kitchen door. And they still loved each other more every day. Only his wrinkles and gray hair were different from their first Christmas together.

Of course, she didn't look the same either. Her hair had turned white years ago. Her hands had spots on them. Her breasts were a little lower. Okay, a lot lower, but her husband didn't seem to mind so she decided not to either. It wasn't like he was *all* the same either. But they had decided to enjoy growing old together and they weren't done yet. In fact, after a round of grandbaby birthdays in January, they were headed to the beach—clothing optional. They would never tell their kids that, though! She loved the shocked expression on her sons' faces and the gasps from her daughter when they caught her and Jake getting frisky in the kitchen.

Way down at the other end of the table, Jake sat with a glass of wine in hand. The table had been expanded twice over the years. For Davies family get-togethers, it now stretched well into the living room. Her children still sat in the same places at the table as they did growing up. But now they had spouses and children filling up the spaces between them.

It was clear to Marcy that the older girl cousins — Piper, Sydney, Reagan, Riley, Layne, and Sophie — couldn't wait to escape the younger boys. Piper, being the eldest of Pierce and Tammy's four kids, tried to ignore her younger siblings and talk to her cousin, Sophie, Cade and Annie's oldest. At seventeen, Sophie was the leader of the girl cousins and was telling them all about being a senior in high school.

"Grandma, did you make apple pie for Christmas?"

Marcy looked down at the round face of the youngest grandchild. Cassidy, Pierce and Tammy's youngest, was only six years old. She looked the most like Helen out of the whole group and had found a way to wiggle into a deeper part of Marcy's heart.

"Yes, dear. Do you think Dylan will share with you?"

Cassidy wrinkled her nose and shook her head. At twelve, her older brother Dylan was taking after his uncles Miles and Marshall. He had muscles and was over five feet tall already. Dylan didn't share food — he inhaled it. Poor Tammy had had no idea how hard it would be to keep the house in food. Paige, with her two older sons, and Katelyn, with fourteen-year-old Wyatt, had quickly filled her in that it would only get worse.

"But Jace might," Cassidy said of her nine-year old brother. Jace was so kind-hearted that Marcy didn't doubt it for a minute.

"Jaaaace?" Cassidy said with a mischievous little smile. "If you don't finish your pie and I finish mine, can I have what's left over?"

Jace smiled at his little sister. "Sure, squirt." Marcy's heart melted as she knew Jace would purposely leave a couple of bites for his little sister.

The sound of a spoon clinking on a glass got everyone's attention. Jake stood smiling at his family. He moved his eyes over seventeen grandchildren, his sons, his daughter, and their spouses, now as dear to him as his own children. He caught the eye of Cole, who was still such a quiet observer after all these years, and then to his Marcy.

Marcy was still as beautiful as the day they married almost fifty-eight years ago. She smiled as she cut slice after slice of apple pie. Their love had never wavered in all their years together. It had only grown stronger and deeper.

Jake raised his wine glass. "Marcy and I are so glad you could all join us today to celebrate Christmas." Jake put his hand to his head. There was a dull ache. It would snow tonight. "Having you here is better than any Christmas present. I hope as the years continue, and as Ryan and Sophie head off to college next year, we continue to do Christmas as we've done for the past fifty-eight years — together. This holiday is all about family and we are blessed to have such a large and caring one."

Marshall and Katelyn's Wyatt nudged his sister Sydney and smiled. For a younger brother, he was very proud and protective of his sixteen-year-old sister. She'd just been asked to be on the cover of *Teen For Me* magazine. Marshall and Katelyn were still discussing if they'd let her. But considering they asked if Katelyn would be on it with her, and if they'd wear two of Paige's hats, Jake was pretty sure they'd say yes.

"Merry Christmas to our dear family!" Jake ended as the toast was met with laughter, teasing, clinking glasses, and excited pleas for apple pie.

As customary, Marcy began serving the pie and Jake walked into the dining room to give her a kiss before stealing the first piece. Being the husband did have some benefits — even Cassidy's wide begging eyes couldn't trump his wife's apple pie and the kiss he got along with it.

Soon the tables were filled with silence as everyone ate apple pie. Jace smiled at his little sister. "Wow. I'm stuffed. Cassidy, can you eat this last part for me?"

His sister's eyes got as big as the grin on her face. "Sure can. Thanks, Jace. You're the best big brother ever."

"Hey. What about me?" Dylan asked.

"Don't you bribe her with pie," Piper teased.

Tammy and Pierce looked over the heads of their children and smiled at each other. They were their own little Davies family now. They'd done a lot over the years, but nothing was as impressive as the four kids sitting between them, not even the Cropbot or the new irrigation system Pierce had developed over the past five years.

Paige looked across the table at her youngest brother and thought about pegging him with a dinner roll like he used to do to her, but she was afraid Greer and Jackson would happily join in and start a food fight. Ryan was trying to be too cool for things like that, but she'd caught him giving Greer a piggyback ride the other day.

Cole and Paige's older boys, seventeen-year-old Ryan and fourteen-year-old Jackson, thought their nine-year-old sister was pretty cool. They didn't think that way until this summer though. Greer had picked up Jackson's bow and arrow, and with a little help from Paige, could now outshoot them in target practice.

After having trouble conceiving, Annie and Cade had all but given up trying. That's when they got Colton who was turning nine next week and less than a year later, they welcomed Landon.

Not wanting to break the pattern they started so many Christmases ago, Paige gave birth to her only girl, Greer, on the same day Annie had Colton. Over the years, Ryan and Sophie, who both had Christmas birthdays, had tried to tell Greer and Colton how cool it was to share a birthday with their cousin. But Colton didn't want to share it with a *girl* at his age.

"You think Katelyn will let Sydney be on that cover?" Cole asked quietly.

"She will. She's already talked to me about the hats," Paige whispered back. Her hat business had grown over the years. Cole was still happy at the FBI in Lexington and they didn't have any plans to change, although she was having a hard time accepting Ryan was heading off to college next year.

"Dad. Talk to Mom, please?" Sydney begged.

"This is between you and your mother. You know I hate the idea. It's bad enough your mom let you start dating this year. Thank goodness I still have a gun. If you and your mom get on that magazine cover, I'll have hordes of pimply squeaky boys at my door," Marshall told her.

Sydney rolled her eyes and Wyatt snickered. "What are you laughing at? You're a pimply squeaker yourself."

"At least I don't make faces in the mirror all afternoon."

"I'm practicing!"

"Practicing looking silly," Wyatt snorted.

"Okay, you two. That's enough. Wyatt, support your

sister. Sydney, don't torture your brother." Katelyn said even though she was talking to Morgan. Marshall just shook his head. He didn't know how she knew all that was going on while carrying on a conversation with someone else. It was some magical mom power.

"Don't laugh, Miles," Katelyn said to her brother-in-law. "Look at Layne. It won't be long before you get to deal with this, too."

Miles sat with his fifteen-year-old daughter, Layne, between him and his wife, Morgan. Layne, as well as all of the grandchildren, had inherited Jake and Helen's hazel eyes. Layne's glowed in anger at her twin eight-year-old boy cousins, Porter and Parker. Cy and Gemma's second set of twins were harassing her about cutting her jet-black hair to impress some boy.

"I did not!" Layne yelled across the table.

"Layne has a boooyfrrrriend," they taunted before their fifteen-year-old twin sisters, Reagan and Riley, smacked the back of their heads.

"It looks great, Layne. Don't listen to those brats."

"Reagan, don't say mean things about your brothers. Someday you'll love them," Gemma said for the hundredth time.

Miles shook his head. His brown hair had gray at the temples now. He'd gotten it when he turned fifty a couple of years back. "Nope. I got a plan for that. I'm locking her in the basement until she's thirty."

Katelyn, Morgan, and Layne all rolled their eyes at him. They all thought he was joking. He had been until a boy had called the house the other day wanting to talk to Layne.

"Don't worry, Layne. Your aunts and I will make sure he'll let you out once or twice a year," Morgan teased.

Over the years together, she and Miles had become

centered. They'd done that to each other. The anxiety and demons of the past had been buried. Now there was laughter and happiness. Even when they'd been unable to have any more children, it had only brought them closer as a family. Now that Morgan was also on the other side of fifty, they accepted it was just the three of them. Layne was their light and they were at every sporting event, every debate, and every choir performance. They loved every moment. They wouldn't change their life for anything.

Cy tossed an anxious look to Gemma. "You'll visit me in jail, right?"

Gemma looked up from where she was telling Porter and Parker to eat their pie rather than smear it on each other. "Cy, we've talked about this. It's no big deal. You did it when you where their age."

"I know," Cy grumbled, "Which is why I know Reagan and Riley should be in the basement with Layne."

Gemma just shook her head as their daughters groaned, "Dad."

"Honey, are you happy? Have you eaten your pie?"

"Yes," Cy answered contentedly.

"Good. I've agreed to let the twins go out with a bunch of other kids to the movies next week," Gemma said calmly.

"What?!" Cy shot up from the table. "Give me their names, social security numbers — no, never mind, I don't need social security numbers. Names and birthdates, now!"

"Cyland Davies!" Marcy scolded. "Your daughters are more than capable of going out in a group." Turning to her granddaughters, Marcy asked, "Reagan, what do you do if a boy pushes for a kiss that you don't want?"

"Tell him no," Reagan said around a bite of pie.

"And if he doesn't take no for an answer?" Marcy

pressed.

"Kick him in the balls," Reagan responded.

"Right. And if he really won't take no for an answer or you can't kick him in the balls, what do you do, Riley?"

"Knock him out with a well-placed punch to the jaw, temple, or back of the head," Riley answered as Aunt Annie gave her a thumbs-up.

"Layne, if someone is doing something you're not comfortable with, what do you do?" Marcy continued to ask.

"Call my dad. If he's not home, my mom. And if I can't get them, then you and Grandpa or any of my aunts and uncles. But I'd probably call Uncle Ahmed first. The kids are scared of him the most."

"They're more scared of him than me?" Cy asked, slightly wounded.

Layne nodded. "And Aunt Annie. She scares them. They heard rumors of the things she used to do with Aunt Bridget."

Annie looked proud as Miles and Cy looked resigned. The cousins looked at each other with triumph in their eyes. They had won the first dating battle.

The conversation around Annie took over. The group talked about dating, boys, girls, teenagers, and driving. Gone were the days where it was talk of dark things such as drugs, dog fighting, and terrorists. A part of her longed to kick a little ass, but she was secure in the fact that she'd taught Sophie everything she knew.

Annie leaned over to Cade and he put his arm around her. Annie grinned to herself. Predictable. He thought she wanted to snuggle. Instead, Annie stabbed her fork into his pie and ate a huge piece.

"Sucker," she said as she chewed.

"You think after almost eighteen years I haven't caught on to your tricks? Isn't that cute?" Cade laughed as his wife wrinkled her nose.

"Ew. I bet they're going to kiss again," Colton said to Landon.

Sophie wrinkled her nose just like her mother. "Not again!"

The brothers and Cole all shared an amused look and then kissed their wives soundly to the sound of their kids' disgust.

Jake looked at his amused wife and smiled. This was all because of them. It was evidence of their love for each other and for their family. The adults laughed and the kids grumbled at seeing their parents kiss.

Not to be left out, Jake stood and walked down the long table to his wife. He held out his hand and Marcy placed hers in it. He helped her out of the chair and pulled her close to him. Jake felt as though there was a permanent indentation on his shoulder where her head fit perfectly.

Marcy leaned her head back and her eyes sparkled with amusement. He lowered his head and kissed her. His hands slid down and gave her bottom a nice pat before bending her back to deepen the kiss.

He could hear his children, now ranging from fifty-two-year-old Miles to forty-one-year-old Pierce groaning. And they thought they could gross out their kids with a little kiss at the table. Amateurs.

Marcy tried not to laugh as her own children made throwing-up noises. Reluctantly, she broke the kiss when the doorbell rang and the door opened. Will and Kenna came in carrying presents. Their daughter, Sienna, was back from her first semester at college and Carter was close behind, not wanting to leave his sister's side. Kenna had told them that Carter had been so glad when Sienna left. That sentiment lasted a week. Now the siblings video-chatted together more than Sienna did with her parents.

"How is college going?" Sophie asked as she pushed past a starry-eyed Ryan.

"Great. I won the Powder Puff football tournament. I still think I should have tried out for the football team, but the guys would have freaked a little. They're such wimps when it comes to playing with a girl."

"I can't wait to go to college. Tell me all about it." Sophie and Sienna headed for the couch with the rest of the girls close behind to talk as Mo and Dani stepped inside the door.

"Zain! Gabe!" Wyatt, Jackson, and Carter called out. The boys ran to see the dark-haired, blue-eyed twins.

"We are so glad to be here. Since Grandfather passed away two years ago, Uncle Dirar has been making us go to Rahmi to learn about being princes and kings," Zain complained as he put some presents under the tree.

"Yeah," Gabe continued. "He says because his son will someday be king, we're like the backups."

Mo shook his head. "It's not that bad."

Dani raised her eyebrows. "I distinctly remember you running from Rahmi to set up your farm here. But, they only have to go over during the summer until they're eighteen. So just two more years."

"It would be a lot cooler if they let us explore and do the things we want instead of prince summer school. Really, am I ever going to need to know who ruled Rahmi in

1267?"

"But if you don't make it through classes, Grandma Fatima won't give you treats," Mo reminded them.

"True," Zain admitted grudgingly.

"Tell me about the new horses you have in Rahmi," Carter asked as the boys broke off from the younger ones.

"Mrs. Davies," Ariana, Mo and Dani's nine-year-old miracle daughter, said as she stood shyly in front of Marcy. Dani had gotten pregnant with Ariana after three miscarriages. She went into pre-term labor at thirty-two weeks. Ariana was born weighing just three and a half pounds. But she was a fighter and came home a month later to be completely spoiled by her whole family.

"Yes, sweetheart?" Marcy replied.

"Did you save any apple pie for me?"

"I sure did. I saved two slices in the kitchen for you and Kale. Speaking of which, here he is."

Ariana smiled and left to drag Ahmed and Bridget's eight-year-old son to the kitchen for pie.

Ahmed kissed her cheek and Marcy flushed. He was a year older than Miles, but Ahmed, like her son, was still just as good-looking. His black hair was still mostly dark. A sliver of gray was brave enough to venture forth in a couple of places. He still looked just as deadly as he had been as the head of security for Mo and the Rahmi royal family. But the darkness that had been in his eyes was now gone. Now they showed joy, love, and peace.

"How is the most beautiful woman in all of Keeneston?"

Marcy swatted his arm. "I think your wife would have something to say if she heard you flirting with me. So would Jake. So let's just not tell them," Marcy giggled.

"Ah, here is my beautiful wife now. Bridget, darling, is Abigail settled?"

Bridget looked over to where their twelve-year-old daughter sat with her leg propped up. All the kids surrounded her as she told them how she broke her leg.

"She's soaking up the attention."

"Oh my goodness! What happened?" Marcy asked.

"You know how she's determined to keep up with the boys. Well, she wanted to enter this martial arts tournament. We told her not to. She was too advanced for them, but she wanted to do it anyway. She entered and won the girls' division easily. When she was sparring with the winner of the boys' division, he got mad she was beating him so easily and did an illegal low kick and fractured her leg. She only has to wear the cast a couple of weeks."

"How horrible."

"All I can say is thank goodness Ahmed kept his hands on his diplomatic immunity papers."

"Me? You're the one who raced across . . ."

"Enough of that!" Bridget said cheerfully, effectively cutting him off. "Anyway, thank you so much for having us over every year."

"You're family," Marcy said as Jake came and put his arm around her.

Bridget and Ahmed joined the group in the living room. The men started to move the table and chairs so everyone could fit. Soon the whole room was filled with people and Christmas cheer.

"We've done well, haven't we?" Jake asked.

Marcy saw the kids playing, the men sharing stories, and the women laughing. "Yes, we have. I can't wait to see what else we do."

Jake raised his drink, "Merry Christmas, everyone!"

"Merry Christmas!"

The End

About the Author

Kathleen Brooks is a New York Times, Wall Street Journal, and USA Today bestselling author. Kathleen's stories are romantic suspense featuring strong female heroines, humor, and happily-ever-afters. Her Bluegrass Series and follow-up Bluegrass Brothers Series feature small town charm with quirky characters that have captured the hearts of readers around the world.

Kathleen is an animal lover who supports rescue organizations and other non-profit organizations such as Friends and Vets Helping Pets whose goals are to protect and save our four-legged family members.

Email Notice of New Releases:
www.kathleen-brooks.com/new-release-notifications/

Kathleen's Website:
www.kathleen-brooks.com

Facebook Page:
www.facebook.com/KathleenBrooksAuthor

Twitter:
www.twitter.com/BluegrassBrooks

Goodreads:
www.goodreads.com/author/show/5101707.Kathleen_Brooks

Other Books by Kathleen Brooks

More Women of Power stories are coming soon! More information will be available shortly on my webpage. The anticipated release for Allegra's story will be in January of 2015 and Mallory's story will hopefully be around April/May of 2015.

There will also be a collection of Rose Sister novellas in mid 2015. A next-generation Bluegrass series will begin sometime in 2015 as well. So much to read in the next year!

Sign up at this link to receive notification for all new releases by Kathleen Brooks: www.kathleen-brooks.com/new-release-notifications/

If you are new to the writings of Kathleen Brooks, then you will definitely want to try her Bluegrass Series books set in the wonderful fictitious town of Keeneston, KY. Here is a list of links to the Bluegrass and Bluegrass Brothers books in order:

Bluegrass Series

Bluegrass State of Mind

Risky Shot

Dead Heat

Bluegrass Brothers Series

Bluegrass Undercover

Rising Storm

Secret Santa, A Bluegrass Novella

Acquiring Trouble

Relentless Pursuit

Secrets Collide

Final Vow

Bluegrass Singles

All Hung Up

Bluegrass Dawn

Women of Power Series

Chosen for Power

Built for Power

Fashioned for Power – coming January 2015

Destined for Power – coming April/May of 2015

Made in United States
Orlando, FL
17 July 2024